GLOOM TOWN

GLOOM TOWN

· RONALD L. SMITH ·

CLARION BOOKS
HOUGHTON MIFFLIN HARCOURT
BOSTON   NEW YORK

Clarion Books
3 Park Avenue
New York, New York 10016

Clarion Books is an imprint of Houghton Mifflin Harcourt Publishing
Company.

hmhbooks.com

The text was set in Janson MT Std.
Chapter opener illustrations by Celeste Knudsen

Library of Congress Cataloging-in-Publication Data
Names: Smith, Ronald L. (Ronald Lenard), 1959– author.
Title: Gloom town / Ronald L. Smith.
Description: Boston ; New York : Clarion Books, 2020. |
Summary: Twelve-year-old Rory and his friend Izzy try to foil the plans
of Lord Foxglove, for whom Rory works as a valet, and his inhuman
accomplices from taking over the world.
Identifiers: LCCN 2019004986 (print) | LCCN 2019012809 (ebook) |
ISBN 9780358164494 (E-book) | ISBN 9781328841612 (hardback)
Subjects: | CYAC: Magic — Fiction. | Household employees—Fiction. |
Shadows — Fiction. | Single-parent families — Fiction. | Poverty—Fiction. |
Horror stories. | BISAC: JUVENILE FICTION / Fantasy & Magic. |
JUVENILE FICTION / Horror & Ghost Stories. | JUVENILE FICTION /
Action & Adventure / Pirates. | JUVENILE FICTION / Family / General
(see also headings under Social Issues).
Classification: LCC PZ7.1.S655 (ebook) | LCC PZ7.1.S655 Glo 2020 (print) |
DDC [Fic]—dc23
LC record available at https://lccn.loc.gov/2019004986

Printed in the United States of America
DOC 10 9 8 7 6 5 4 3 2 1
4500788185

For Harriet, who always believed

CONTENTS

GLOOM TOWN

A Town Called Gloom

The town was called Gloom, which was a strange name for a town, but if you ever found yourself there, you would certainly see why. Some said that merchant sailors gave it the name long ago, when they pulled their ships into the harbor only to be met by wind, rain, and very little sunlight.

But that's an old tale, and no one knows for sure anymore.

In the midst of all this gloom, there lived a boy named Rory. He wasn't the happiest boy in the world, but he often found small joys in life, like discovering a silver stone by the water's edge, playing with his friend Izzy, and, every now and then, swimming in Quintus Harbor, even though his mum told him not to.

His ordinary life was soon about to change. In ways he never could have imagined.

CHAPTER ONE

Mr. Bumbailiff

The knocking is what first roused Rory from sleep, a furious banging on the front door loud enough to wake the dead.

Rory knew that sound. It came from a heavy walking stick, one with a knob of gnarled wood on the end of it the size of a swollen walnut. Only one person used a stick like that.

He threw on his shirt and pants and rushed out of his room. His mum had already opened the door to reveal a large man dressed in a dirty plaid suit of red and green. His face was a lesson in scowling. A black bowler hat sat on top of his head.

"Rent," he said brusquely.

Rory's mum, whose name was Hilda Sorenson, feigned a smile—although if you knew her well enough you could hear her voice tremble. "Do come in, good sir. I'll fetch you a cup of tea."

The man, who was known as Mr. Bumbailiff, snorted once and stepped into the small house. Rory's mum closed the door behind him and turned to her son. "Rory, some tea for our guest, yeah?"

Mr. Bumbailiff propped his walking stick against the side of a chair and sat down heavily. He glared at Rory as if waiting to be served. Rory grudgingly walked to the shabby kitchen and lit the coal stove, then put the kettle on.

It was a modest house with a sitting room in the front with a fireplace and an old piano, a kitchen in the back, and two tiny rooms upstairs. There wasn't a bathroom, but a big copper tub sat in the kitchen for washing up. Unfortunately, they had to go outside to use what they called a privy. Rory didn't like it, but it was all they had. Most of the people in Gloom didn't have running water and had to use a well or one of the water pumps placed around town. Rory and his mum were lucky. Their house was right next to a pump, so it wasn't too much trouble getting water to bathe in. But they still had to heat the water in a big pot on the stove first. All in all, living in Gloom wasn't terribly comfortable.

Rory returned to the sitting room and sat down next to his mum on a well-worn couch.

"Well," Mr. Bumbailiff said, peering around with an air of authority. "Place looks a bit shabby." He ran a stubby finger across the armrest of the wooden chair he sat in. "Your lease states that the house must be kept free of dust and dirt at all times."

"Yes, yes," Rory's mum said quickly, wringing her red-knuckled hands. "It's just with my hours at the inn and the tannery, it's hard to find extra time to clean."

The landlord looked at Rory derisively. "What about him? He's a big lad. Surely he knows how to wield a broom."

Rory swallowed a curse in his throat. He had survived several visits from the landlord before and had always ignored his snide remarks. But today, Rory didn't like the way the man made his mum cower in front of him. She was almost shaking with dread. They'd been late with the rent for the past two months, and now there were no more excuses. They needed money, and quickly.

The teapot whistled from the kitchen, but before Rory could get up to tend it, Mr. Bumbailiff glanced at his watch and then stood. "Never mind the tea," he said. "I have a full schedule today and I can't be running late." He paused and raised a bushy eyebrow. "So . . . the rent."

"Yes," Hilda said. "One moment." She looked to her son, and Rory saw that her eyes were wet. "Rory?"

Rory ground his teeth. He hated seeing his mum humiliated like this. With a withering glance at Mr. Bumbailiff, he stood up and walked back to the kitchen. He took the kettle from the stove and set it on an iron trivet, then removed a framed painting from the wall and placed it on the table. The picture was of no consequence, only a muddy watercolor of Quintus Harbor at dawn, but behind it, there was a loose brick. Rory pulled it out with a scrape and set it next to the painting. He reached inside the dark hole and retrieved the money jar, then opened it up and counted. They were short, but it would have to do. There was no other way around it.

Back in the sitting room, Rory stood in front of the landlord. He wanted to throw the money in his scowling face but instead held it out to him, as if offering a slice of cake. "Here you are, sir."

Mr. Bumbailiff snatched the bills from Rory's hand. Now Rory really wanted to punch him. The landlord raised his right hand to his mouth and licked his thumb. "One," he said, counting the first bill. "Two . . . "

A minute later, after he had counted the last bill, he released a heavy sigh. "Seems you're still a bit short," he said, then looked to Hilda. "I'm afraid I can't extend my generosity any further. You'll have to pack your things. You have till tomorrow morning."

Rory's mouth dropped open. His mum stared at the floor, defeated. She seemed suddenly so much smaller to Rory at that moment, like she had shrunk into herself.

Rory bit back his anger. "Please, sir. We can get the rest. I promise. Just another few days and we'll be all square."

Now, as Rory said this, he had no idea where he was going to get the money, but he had to do something. Anything. His mum raised her head and glanced at him. "He's right," she said, holding back tears. "Just another few days. I'll get another shift at the inn. You'll see. Just a few more days, good sir."

Mr. Bumbailiff was now in his element. He seemed to enjoy making people squirm. He stuck his thumbs in his suspenders and leaned back a bit. "A few days, you say?"

"Yes," Rory and his mum said at the same time.

The landlord exhaled a wheezy, rattling breath. "One

week," he declared. "With interest. If not, you're out. Do you understand?"

"Yes," Hilda said. "Thank you, sir. We won't let you down."

Mr. Bumbailiff shook his head and picked up his walking stick. Rory wanted to clobber him with it. The landlord turned for the door, then slammed it shut behind him without so much as a backward glance. The sound echoed in the air for what seemed like minutes.

Rory's mum turned to him, her eyes red-rimmed.

"What do we do now?" she said.

CHAPTER TWO

Rory Devises a Plan

"That's everything," Rory's mum moaned. "All our money. Gone."

Rory sat down next to her on the couch. Dull afternoon light drifted in through the window.

"It's okay, Mum," he consoled her. "I'll think of something."

"But what?" Hilda questioned. "You're too young to work on the ships. That's all the work there is in this awful town."

It was true, Rory knew.

In Gloom, most boys and girls worked on the ships that set sail from the docks at Quintus Harbor—cleaning and scrubbing the decks, sewing sailcloth, and working their way up to becoming riggers, who were in charge of furling and releasing the sails. But Rory was only twelve—thirteen in a few short weeks—and the rules said you had to be at least fourteen years of age to work. Rory had no idea who came up with the rules or how they were even enforced. He knew a boy once named Petru who worked on the ships when he was only eleven years old. He was tall for his age, though, and his father just happened to be a quartermaster. *Come to think of it,* Rory mused, *that must've been the reason.*

"I'll find a job," he said. "Promise."

Hilda Sorenson pulled a cloth from her dress pocket and blew her nose. It was as loud as a honking goose.

Rory laid a comforting hand on her shoulder, which she clasped in return.

"All is not lost yet," she said. She rose from the couch and smoothed her wrinkled dress with her hands, then bent back down to the floor. A loose slat of wood creaked as she pulled it up. Underneath was a small glittering mound.

"Where'd that come from?" Rory asked in surprise.

"I saved it," his mum replied, standing. "Just enough to buy us a few days if we ever fell behind."

She counted out several shiny coins and handed them to Rory. "Run to the market and get enough food for the week. Spend it wisely. No cakes or pies. Understand?"

"Right," Rory said reluctantly.

Without warning, she threw her arms around him and held him tight. "It'll be all right, Son," she said. "We'll be okay."

"I know, Mum," he replied, his eyes stinging. "I know."

Outside, Rory passed the belching factories and foundries on Copper Street. Small, low houses and bleak taverns dotted the landscape. The smell of iron forges and the clanging of smiths hard at work could be heard in the distance. Specks of black dust floated in the air around him.

Rory lived here, along with a few hundred other unfortunate souls. It was one of the poorest neighborhoods in Gloom, but it was all he and his mum could afford. Most people didn't come to Copper Street unless they wanted trouble. Roving gangs armed with brass knuckles and blunderbusses were known to prowl the streets late at night, looking for easy victims. "Marks," the villains called them. Rory didn't want to be a mark, so he kept a brisk pace and tucked his chin. But that wasn't strange. Everyone in Gloom walked like that.

Rory took in the sights as he went about his way, but there really wasn't much to see. The town was situated alongside Quintus Harbor, which fed into the Black Sea. He stopped by the docks for a moment and watched men and women unloading nets of fish from their boats. White gulls and other seabirds hovered in the air around them, hoping to snag a tasty morsel. The sailors were hard people—wind chafed and grim from spending their lives on the water. The bounty they usually brought in was tremendous: huge sea crabs and scallops; eels, urchins, cod, and shrimp. Rory, and every other person in Gloom, grew up on food from the sea. They ate so much that folks far and wide said their blood was made of salt water.

Every now and then, Rory and his best friend, Izzy, would sit on the docks and stare out over the bay. Once, they saw a fighting ship far in the distance, its massive sails snapping in the breeze. Rory loved ships and often fantasized about sailing and adventure. Of course, he was always the hero in these stories, most of them having to do with battling giant squids and visiting far-off lands. As he'd looked out over the water that day, he wondered who was on that ship and where they were going. From time to time, people in Gloom spoke of war in a faraway land, but Rory didn't know anything about that. He figured they were just making up stories to explain things they didn't really understand.

After a few more minutes of walking, he arrived at Market Square, an outdoor space open year round, where vendors' stalls lined the perimeter. To the east of the square, tall trees stood at the edge of the forest known as the Glades, another favorite haunt of Izzy and Rory's.

Even though it was midmorning, a pallid grayness hung over the town, courtesy of the foggy marine layer that rolled in daily. It usually took several hours for it to clear, and the fog seemed to seep into everything, which made Gloom even gloomier.

The square was bustling with vendors selling everything from fish to bread to oysters to clams. Rory bought two speckled trout, a jug of milk, a loaf of crusty bread, and a packet of salt. He still had two coppers left. He licked his lips at a stall called Miss Julia's that sold pies and sweets. Rory loved a bit of sweet after a meal, but they couldn't afford it. He sighed and lifted his pack over his shoulder. Before he turned to leave the square and make his way back home, a handbill pasted to a lamppost caught his eye. Rory leaned in to read it:

Gentleman's Valet needed at Foxglove Manor for duties
befitting the title.
Must be familiar with the tools of the trade.
Pay requisite with experience.
333 Mothsburg Lane

Rory's pulse raced. Here was a job he could do. He didn't exactly know what a valet was or what the tools of the trade were, but he was sure he could figure it out. He was smart like that. There was only one problem.

It was at Foxglove Manor.

Everyone in Gloom had heard of the place. It had been in the town for generations and was the source of incredible tales and rumors. People said it was haunted by the spirits of previous tenants, that it had rooms that appeared and disappeared at will, and, most frightful of all, that you could be turned to ash just by stepping inside.

But Rory didn't believe any of those things. The people of Gloom were a superstitious lot, and the first to blame bogies and spirits for the most easily explained events. Truth be told, it was probably the dark clouds that hung over the town year after year that caused this malaise. It was part of Gloom. It was *in* Gloom.

"A job," Rory whispered. "Money to help Mum and me."

He tore the handbill from the pole and raced home.

Rory rushed into the house out of breath and waving the handbill. "A job!" he cried out. "For a gentleman's valet at Foxglove Manor!"

He set down his pack on the table. His mum was in front

of the fire, drinking a cup of tea. She got up and turned to him. Rory could tell she had been crying. Her face was splotchy and wet. "At Foxglove Manor?" she asked warily.

Rory handed her the notice and watched as she read it. "Seems on the up-and-up," she said, handing it back. "But—"

Rory raised an eyebrow. "You don't believe all that stuff about the manor, do you, Mum?"

Hilda sat back down by the fire, and Rory took a seat in one of the chairs beside her.

"No," she said, "not really. I'm sure it's all just rubbish."

But Rory saw concern etched on her face. She wasn't sure about it.

"We *need* the money," he said urgently. "If I get the job, we won't have to worry about Mr. Bumbailiff, at least for a while."

Hilda took out her handkerchief and dabbed her eyes.

Rory was taken aback. "What is it, Mum? What's wrong?"

"This shouldn't all fall on you, Son." She sniffed. "You should be out enjoying being a boy, not worrying about whether you have a roof over your head."

"But it's not all on me," Rory countered. "You work two jobs every day, Mum. It's only fair I do my part as well."

Hilda turned to him. She clasped his hand. Embers popped and hissed in the fireplace. Rory looked into the flames.

"I'll get the job," he said quietly, "and we'll pay off that miserable Mr. Bumbailiff. Then, maybe we can go on a little trip. Set sail and see all of Europica. How's that sound, Mum?"

In answer, Hilda Sorenson squeezed her son's hand a little more tightly. "That would be splendid, Rory. Absolutely splendid."

CHAPTER THREE

Upon Entering Foxglove Manor

The house itself was a monstrosity—a gargantuan tapestry
of brick, wood, and stone—jutting out of the earth like a
madman's nightmare. It leaned a little, too, as if the whole
thing could blow over in a strong wind. Creeping green vines
snaked their way up the walls and coiled around a crumbling,
blackened chimney.

Rory swallowed hard.

Only a crumbly, old house, he reassured himself.

Mothsburg Lane was east of Copper Street and farther
away from Quintus Harbor. The houses here were set apart
from one another, giving the inhabitants room to breathe. In

15

Rory's neighborhood, most people lived in small row homes crammed together. But not here. Patches of green grass divided the houses, most of which loomed behind high gates and tall trees. Rory wondered how much money it would cost to maintain them. There would have to be a groundskeeper, maids, butlers, and all manner of servants. But he saw no sign of life on the street, not even a stray dog or a slinky, roaming cat, which were numerous around Copper Street and Market Square—closer to the docks and scraps of food, he figured.

He let out a breath. What would Izzy say if she saw him here now? He needed to tell her about the job he was seeking. She was his best friend after all.

Rory walked up a row of white steps and faced the door. He'd wanted to arrive early that morning, but he'd had chores around the house to finish first. Now it was already late afternoon. *A gentleman's valet,* he thought again. That was a butler of sorts. Someone who helped rich people do stuff. *I can do that,* he told himself. *How hard could it be?*

Rory took a deep breath and reached for the door knocker. He shivered. It was a gruesome, leering face, the tongue being the knocker itself. He picked it up and let it fall, sending an echo down the block and back again.

The air was cool, and red and gold leaves swirled around

on the stoop. The glass in the gaslight above his head was shattered. The air smelled like copper pennies.

He shuffled his feet. *Why is it taking so long?*

The heavy door opened with a creak.

A man in a black and white butler's uniform stood before him. He was very tall and stooped, as if he had trouble straightening himself. His arms hung at his sides like some sort of simian creature.

Rory didn't speak while the butler looked him up and down. Finally, he realized he should say something first. "My name's Rory," he said a little too quickly, "and I'm here about the gentleman's valet job."

The butler continued to observe him, and Rory noticed that one eye was blue and the other ice-cold gray, which Rory found quite unsettling. Long, dark hair hung flat on either side of his face.

"Are you indeed?" the butler asked in a deep, slow voice, his mouth opening and closing like a marionette.

"Am I indeed what?" Rory asked.

"Why, a gentleman's valet," the man answered, as if Rory was the dumbest boy in the world.

"Oh," Rory replied, trying to put on a good face. "Yes, well. I suppose so."

The butler let out a dismissive *humph,* then straightened a little and pulled the door wide. "Follow me," he said.

And that's what Rory did.

He found himself in a long, narrow hall, with rooms to either side. Decorative brass sconces were affixed to the walls, spreading weak light. He had heard of gaslight inside homes before but had never been in one that had it. Paintings were hung close together in ornate frames of gold and silver. There were so many that Rory could barely make out the color of the wall beneath. They were all portraits—men and women looking out from their frames with solemn gazes. They seemed to be from another era, one Rory was not familiar with—men with powdered wigs and ruffled collars, women with elaborate hairstyles and glittering jewels around their necks. Rory took it all in quickly, trying not to ogle at the strangeness he had just stepped into. At the end of the hall, a rusted suit of armor stood at the ready, silver lance in hand.

The butler made a right turn and Rory followed. The room they entered was like nothing he had ever seen. Tall windows let in light through faded yellow curtains. One wall revealed a towering bookshelf sagging under the weight of too many leather-bound books. Fancy chairs with scrolled armrests and clawed feet were spread about, and several candelabras sat on tables and pedestals. Paintings were hung here as well, but not as many as in the hall.

"Please," the butler said. "Take a seat."

Rory looked left, then right. He wasn't sure where to sit but finally settled in a chair covered in a mossy-green fabric. A lighted candelabra flickered on a small table beside him. The man remained standing, reached within his suit jacket, and took out a small pad of paper and a black fountain pen. He flipped to a blank page, coughed, and then said, "Diseases. Do you have any?"

Rory swallowed. His mum told him he'd once had the ague when he was very little. Is that what the man meant? But he didn't have time to answer.

"Have you ever been to Outer Europica?" The butler continued.

"No," Rory answered.

"The Isle of Falling Clouds?"

"No."

"Have you ever seen a snake shed its skin?"

"No."

"Been bitten by a tarantula?"

"No."

"Have you ever found a golden egg?"

Golden egg? Rory thought. *What is this all about?*

"No, sir," he said. "I'm here about the job. The valet job."

The butler looked up from his pad. His gray eye moved around in its socket, while the blue one remained still. "Why, what do you think we are doing, young man? This is an interview. Lord Foxglove is taking great care with whom he shall hire for the position."

"Lord Foxglove?"

The butler closed his eyes and then sighed. "This house is called Foxglove Manor, is it not?" He didn't wait for an answer. "That means, quite possibly, that someone by that name might *reside* here. Do you understand?"

Rory swallowed. "Yes."

This interview wasn't going very well.

The man turned away and walked to the bookcase. He rubbed his chin, then extended a long finger and pulled a book from the shelf. Rory watched him as he turned and made his way back. He had a strange gait, more animal than human, almost as if he were walking on his tiptoes. He stopped in front of Rory and handed him the book. The cover was dusty, and Rory felt his nose tingle as if he were about to sneeze, but somehow he avoided it.

"Can you read?" the butler asked.

"Yes," Rory answered. Reading was one of his favorite pastimes, though good books were hard to come by in Gloom. They were all sad stories with unhappy endings.

"Very well," the man replied. "Open to any page and read a passage."

Rory shifted in his seat. He felt a coiled spring underneath him and thought it would burst through and poke his backside. *Why does he want me to do that?* Maybe he'd have to read shopping and errand lists for Lord Foxglove if he was hired. He couldn't think of any other reason.

"Ahem," the butler sniffed, impatient.

Rory looked at the cover. Words in an unknown language stared back at him. Maybe it was different inside, he thought, and opened the book. The butler crouched down, close to Rory's face. Rory caught a faint whiff of something unpleasant. He wrinkled his nose.

"Anywhere will do," the man instructed him.

Rory scanned down the page, which seemed to be some kind of brittle parchment. He exhaled. "The ancient sea mariners of old crafted ships from the finest ebony—"

"That's enough." The butler cut him off and rose back up to his full height.

Rory closed the book. Dust coated his fingertips.

A sly grin formed on the strange man's face. "You didn't say you could read Old Aramaic."

"Old *what?*"

"Aramaic, one of the oldest languages in the world."

"Well, I can't," Rory said rather bluntly.

"Well, you just did, young man. You just did." He crouched down again, and Rory saw a long, black hair curling out of one nostril. "And how, pray tell, do you explain that?"

Rory gulped. "Luck?"

His interviewer straightened back up. Rory wanted to check the book again and get a closer look, but it was quickly snatched away.

"Lord Foxglove has charged me with finding a valet." The butler sniffed. "You'll do."

Rory contained his excitement. He had a job!

"Come back tomorrow and the lord of the manor will take a look at you." The butler reached into his suit jacket and took out a scroll of paper, which unspooled to the floor like a ribbon. "It's all in order," he said, handing Rory his fountain pen. "Please sign."

Rory held the heavy pen between his fingers. *Take a look at me?* he thought. *What did he mean by that?*

Rory lifted the bottom of the page and brought it close

to his face. Several passages were written in English, as well as other languages he didn't recognize. It was as if a colony of ants had swarmed the page. "What exactly am I signing?" he asked.

"I thought you said you could read," the butler scolded. "You are signing a contract, and in order to do that, one must be able to read, don't you think? That is why I asked you in the first place."

A contract, Rory thought. He had never signed anything before, especially something as important looking as this. He tried to focus. He had a decision to make. He and his mum needed money, that was certain, but he didn't know what all of these words meant. *Just do it,* he told himself. Mr. Bumbailiff's threat rang in his ears: *One week . . . with interest. If not, you're out.*

Rory steeled himself, and then signed on the dotted line.

The butler quickly snatched the paper from his hands. It was only then that Rory saw, very clearly, as if it had just come into focus, a few words in a small, fanciful script at the bottom of the page, and they struck him like an arrow:

Upon Penalty of Death.

CHAPTER FOUR

Black Maddie's

Rory left Foxglove Manor in a daze. His thoughts were scattered. He knew he had just signed a contract, but the memory of it was floating away second by second, like a dream.

He felt mesmerized. Under a spell. How had he been able to read all of those strange words? The butler had said it was Old Aramaic. How could that be?

And what about Lord Foxglove? Shouldn't Rory have met his employer?

Oh well, he thought, *nothing to do for it now.*

A gray and white cat lazily strolled in front of Rory as he passed Black Maddie's, Gloom's most popular inn. It was a small, one-story building made from white stones covered in slick, wet moss. Loud, raucous music drifted out the door and into the street.

Rory climbed the steps and wiped his muddy shoes on a straw mat. Inside, the strong aroma of beer, smoke, and cooked mutton filled the air. It was a familiar scent and one that clung to his clothes every time he visited. Darkness lay over the place like a cloak but for a few fat candles placed on the square-cut, wooden tables. Music rose above the din of clinking bottles and raised voices. Rory looked to the make-shift stage built with planks of wood stacked higher than the floor. One melancholy voice rose in the air and he smiled. It was his mum, singing a sad sea ballad, one that she had sung to him when he was a child, and he knew the tune well:

> "So I signed aboard a whaling ship
> and my very first day at sea,
> there I spied in the waves,
> her reaching out for me.
> 'Come live with me in the sea,' said she,
> 'down on the ocean floor,
> and I'll show you many a wondrous thing
> that you've never seen before.'"

Hilda Sorenson raised her arms in the air. The pianist, a man as skinny and white as a bleached skeleton, hammered away at the keys. A few strands of lank hair clung to his bald head. Rory shifted his gaze back to his mum. She had bright-red hair that flowed down her back and a thin, sharp nose — two things Rory had not inherited. He was darker than most in Gloom, with close-cropped, curly black hair and almond-shaped eyes. When Rory asked his mum why they looked so different, she'd told him that he favored his father and left it at that. Rory could tell it was something she didn't want to talk about.

His mum stood against a backdrop of a rippling sail-cloth painted sky blue. If you looked at it closely enough, you could imagine seagulls and small white ships riding the waves. After the song was finished, Hilda and Rory sat at a table in the dim back of the room. Rory ordered a cinnamon root elixir from the barkeep. It was his favorite drink. There were certainly stronger cordials available at Black Maddie's, but Rory wasn't of age to drink them. Plus, he didn't want to. More than once, he'd seen the men stumbling out of the inn, their legs too rubbery to hold them up. They usually fell into a heap and didn't move again until morning, when they dusted themselves off and went about their way.

"There's my love." Rory's mum kissed him on the cheek. She had dark circles under her eyes from too many nights singing for tips after working at the leather tannery during the day.

"Well?" she asked eagerly, raising her eyebrows in anticipation.

Rory sipped his drink. He had good news, although the circumstances were still a bit odd to him. He decided to draw out the moment, and slurped again.

"Rory." She persisted.

He set his glass on the table. "I'll be working at Foxglove Manor as a valet."

Hilda Sorenson almost jumped out of her seat, which was quite dramatic for someone who lived in Gloom. "Oh! That's wonderful, my boy! Splendid. Now, tell me all about it. When do you start?"

"Tomorrow." Rory paused.

He had no idea what time he was supposed to show up. All he remembered was that the butler had said to come tomorrow to meet Lord Foxglove. *Take a look at you,* he recalled with a shiver.

"Tomorrow?" Hilda repeated. "Not much time to get ready then, huh?"

Rory shrugged.

"Well," she said optimistically, picking a speck of lint from Rory's frayed sweater. "I've taught you a few things, haven't I? You know how to tie a cravat, mix a whiskey sour, press a shirt, and tell a good joke. So, do you think you're prepared?"

Rory nodded. "I think so."

But inside, he wasn't really sure. He remembered the words on the contract he had just signed: *Upon Penalty of Death.*

He swallowed the last of his drink.

CHAPTER FIVE

Lord Foxglove

Rory woke to the smell of fried bread. His mum must have made him a slice. He dressed quickly and headed downstairs, hoping she was alone.

Sometimes, Rory would wake up to find men and women sprawled on the sitting room floor and furniture. Rory's mum called these people her "comrades" and said they'd been together through thick and thin. There was Vincent, who wore a type of eyeglass called a monocle, a round piece of glass that fit snugly over one eye. He had one leg shorter than the other and walked with an ivory-tipped cane. Ox Bells was as big as a giant, with a gleaming bald head and hands as meaty as two cooked hams. Supposedly, he had once worked as a strongman at a circus, but if there had ever been a circus in Gloom, Rory hadn't heard of it. Then there was Miss Cora, who sported the fanciest clothes Rory had ever seen — long red gloves up to her elbows and hats that were shaped like animals. One time, Rory thought an actual squirrel had taken up residence in her hair but soon learned it was just another one of her hats, a "cloud," she'd called it.

Whenever these comrades visited, Rory's mum referred to their little front room as a *salon*. Rory wasn't sure what that meant. They usually played cards or sang songs around the battered piano late at night. Sad songs, of course, it being Gloom. But last night, the house had been quiet. Rory had slept uneasily, rolling around in his bed. He still had to meet Lord Foxglove, and he had no idea what to expect.

Downstairs in the kitchen, his mum had laid out the toast and two boiled eggs. Rory sat down and dug in. He ate quickly, not even relishing the wonderful taste. He was preoccupied, his brain racing. Tension gnawed in the pit of his stomach. It was the butler. Something wasn't right about him. And Rory was certain it was more than just the man's creepy eyes.

"So," his mum said, sitting across from him. "You have the job, but you haven't met the . . . what's he called?"

"Lord of the manor," Rory reminded her.

"Right. Figured it would be something fancy like that."

"I thought I'd go in early, you know," Rory said between bites. "Make a good impression."

Hilda cocked her head. "They never said what time?"

"No."

"Humph. That's odd."

Rory thought it odd too. But he resisted saying anything about how strange the interview really was. It would only startle her. And he didn't want that, especially with Bumbailiff breathing down their necks.

Rory gulped down the rest of his food.

Before he left, his mum gave him a kiss on the cheek. "For good luck," she said.

Rory hoped he wouldn't need it.

He passed the docks, dodging the frequent droppings from the gulls overhead. The Strasse, the main avenue of Gloom, stretched out before him like a winding snake. It ran from one end of the town to the other. Small shops and homes lined both sides of the street. Rory had taken this route so many times he could navigate it with his eyes closed.

The heavy, gray sky seemed closer to the ground than usual. It had always been dim in Gloom, but lately, it was getting darker earlier and earlier. People went about their tasks as if in a trance—from the fishmonger laying out gleaming, silvery fish to the old woman who sold wilted flowers. Rory felt bad for her. The flowers were just as forlorn as the people in Gloom. No one ever bought any because they were so pitiful, with dull petals and drooping leaves.

Rory turned down Mothsburg Lane and Foxglove Manor came into view. He hadn't noticed before, but there was a balcony on the second floor, with a railing where one could look out over the town. The gray paint was peeling, and the wooden eaves above it were water damaged, revealing mis-shapen islands of green mold.

Rory walked up the steps and faced the frightful knocker again. He took a breath, then lifted the tongue and let it fall. His heart raced. The thought of meeting his new employer had him on edge.

The door opened slowly. It was the butler. He looked just as strange as he had before. "Ah, there he is. I was wondering when you might show."

"I wasn't sure what time to arrive," Rory said, contrite.

The butler frowned. "Taking initiative is a trait Lord Foxglove finds most admirable in young people."

Rory wasn't sure if that was a compliment or not.

The man led him through the reception hall and Rory

glanced at all of the paintings once again. Instead of turning right, as they had before, into the room with all of the books, they continued straight. Rory thought the butler was leading them directly into the wall, but once they passed the suit of armor at the end, another hall came into view on the right. More gas lamps ran along the rose-colored walls, which were adorned with intricate molding and chair rails. They passed a closed door painted deep red, which seemed odd to Rory, as it didn't match the rest of the fancy decor he had seen so far.

"Where are we going?" he asked.

"To meet the lord of the manor, of course."

Rory gulped. He was finally going to meet Lord Foxglove.

The hallway ended at a door. The butler opened it. Rory felt cool air on his face. Spiraling stone steps led down into darkness.

The more they descended, the darker and colder it got. The only thing that kept Rory from stumbling was the hand-rail he instinctively reached out for. Why were there no lights down here, like upstairs? The vague silhouette of the butler loomed in front of him like a floating shadow.

Why would the lord of the manor be down here? Rory wondered.

After a moment, he rounded a final curve of stairs and stepped onto a hard floor. An actual flaming torch affixed to the wall was the only source of light. It seemed to be a sort of entryway or foyer, a word Rory had learned from books.

The butler paused in front of a set of wooden double doors with unusual carvings. Rory glimpsed twisting tree limbs, a flock of shadowy birds in flight, and a woman's face. But before he could study them, his guide spoke.

"Three things," he began, and held up a finger. "One, do not speak unless spoken to." Another finger rose in the air. "Two, always address him as Lord Foxglove. And three, never, under any circumstance, ask about money."

Rory was taken aback. How would he know what he was going to earn if he couldn't ask about his wages?

The double doors groaned on their hinges as the butler pushed them forward.

And then, they both stepped inside.

Rory was immediately hit by a blast of even colder air. There were lanterns that cast a little light, but not enough to brighten the whole room.

He took in the long, rectangular space before him. On one wall, hundreds of bottles of wine were arranged on a rack. Next to it, on an ornate table of glass held aloft by slim brass legs, sat several beautiful decanters filled with murky liquids. *Strange,* Rory thought. *What could that be?* The opposite wall displayed more portraits, just like upstairs, most of them showing men with powdered wigs and ruffled collars. Rory looked down to his feet. The marble floor was a mosaic of black-and-white tiles. His head spun. He felt disoriented for some reason.

"Pardon, my lord," the butler said.

Only then did Rory notice, at the far end of the room, a man sitting behind a massive wooden table littered with stacks of paper, bottles of ink, and other curious objects he couldn't make out.

Rory gasped as the man stood up. He was skinnier and taller than any person he'd ever seen. His head was bald, but he bore a magnificent black beard that rested on his chest. A long, black waistcoat slashed with daggers of red clung to his frame. Underneath was a gleaming white shirt, complete with a gray ascot tucked into the neck. He had an air of stuffiness about him, as if he were royalty or something. He was certainly different from anyone Rory had ever seen in Gloom.

"Ah, Malvonius," Lord Foxglove began. "So this is the boy?"

Rory was almost too shocked by Lord Foxglove's appearance and dress to realize he had just learned the butler's name: Malvonius. *What kind of name is that?*

"It is," the butler answered. "He has . . . accepted the position."

Accepted? Rory thought, but then realized he *had* signed the contract: *Upon Penalty of Death*. He swallowed hard.

"I am pleased to make your acquaintance, Rory," the lord of the manor said, stepping around the desk. His voice wasn't deep nor was it high, but somewhere in between, with a reedy quality to it, as if at any moment he would purse his lips and whistle. His eyes were as cold as ice chips.

Rory was dumbstruck. Was he supposed to bow? Kneel? He wasn't sure. In the end, he gave a solemn nod of his head.

"Do not be afraid, boy," Lord Foxglove said. "Mr. Root has told me all about you."

Root. Malvonius Root. A strange name for sure. And exactly what did this Malvonius tell him?

"Do come closer." Foxglove beckoned, offering an open palm in invitation. "I won't bite."

Malvonius actually chuckled, which sent a shiver down Rory's spine.

Lord Foxglove walked back around to the table, swept his coattails behind him and sat, then waved a big hand to a chair beside him that looked much too large for Rory. "Please. Sit down. Bring us something cool to drink, Malvonius."

Something hot would have been better, Rory figured. It was as cold as an icebox in the room. The butler inclined his head in obedience and turned around.

Rory stepped forward and sat in the chair, his feet hovering a few inches above the floor.

Malvonius returned bearing a silver tray with a crystal pitcher of red liquid and two etched glasses rimmed with hammered-copper bands. He approached and set it down on the table. Rory watched as the butler poured. It looked like blood.

"Ah," Lord Foxglove said, raising his glass. "To your health." Rory followed his lead. He let Foxglove swallow first and then did the same. His mouth soured. It was certainly a different kind of taste—sweet and tart at the same time.

Malvonius retreated toward the door. Rory's new employer set his glass on the table in front of him and leaned back in his chair. He studied Rory intently, and Rory found it hard to hold his gaze. His eyes were a little too pale and odd. Finally, when the silence was almost too much to bear, Lord Foxglove said, "I suppose you want to ask about . . . you know."

Rory bit his lip. He *was* curious. How much was he going to earn? Why was Lord Foxglove so skinny? He had so many questions, but in the end, he only nodded.

Foxglove smiled. "It's pomegranate juice," he said.

Rory looked at the pitcher of red liquid. "Oh."

The lord of the manor threw his head back and laughed. It was a sharp, barking sound that Rory found unsettling.

"Let me ask you," Lord Foxglove said, regaining his composure and steepling his hands together, which revealed several glittering rings, one of them shaped like the head of a snarling wolf. "Are you qualified for the job?"

Rory shifted in his seat. He wanted to appear eager and ready, but his nerves were all jangly. "Yes, sir, and I'm a quick learner, too."

"Good. You will find room and board here, and it will be deducted from your wages." He paused. "A valet has many duties. Do you know what they are?"

Rory wasn't sure. He wanted to bite his fingernails, but that would have made him seem nervous. "Um," he started, but his new boss cut him off.

"Once, this house was full of servants—footmen, scullery maids, butlers—but now those days are gone. Changing times and all."

Rory nodded, as if he understood what it meant to have servants.

Foxglove laid his hands on the table. Rory noticed that

each fingernail ended in a sharp point. "I need someone to take up those duties. Do you understand?"

Rory wasn't sure he did, and his face must have betrayed his thoughts.

"That means sweeping the chimneys, polishing the silver, beating the dust out of the rugs." He paused and sipped his juice. "Now, do you think you can do all that? Are you up to the task?"

"Yes," Rory said immediately. He needed this job more than anything. He had to help his mum.

"Good," Lord Foxglove said. "Very good indeed."

Rory swallowed nervously. He needed to know about wages. But the butler—Malvonius Root—had told him to not ask about money.

Foxglove stood up. "Report here tomorrow morning at half-past eight," he said. "You can begin then."

Rory rose out of his seat. He thought he was starting today. But it didn't matter. He had the job, and that's what counted.

Lord Foxglove reached down, pulled open a drawer in the table, and rummaged around. He drew out a brown leather pouch and held it in front of Rory like a master giving a dog a treat. Rory stuck out his hand hesitantly, palm up.

Time seemed to slow down as the bag dropped. Rory felt the weight of it immediately.

Money.

He wanted to shake it to hear the coins clink but used every ounce of his will not to.

"That should be enough for now," Foxglove said. "There's more where that came from." He leaned down close and lowered his voice. "*If* you do a good job, that is."

Rory couldn't believe it. He could only imagine how much money was in the pouch. "Thank you, sir. I won't let you down."

Lord Foxglove smiled, and for the first time, Rory noticed that his teeth were as sharp as his fingernails.

Outside, Rory stood on the steps. He couldn't even wait to get down the street. He had to know. *Now.*

He opened the drawstring on the pouch and looked inside. He drew in a breath. Silver and gold coins winked in the dim afternoon light. Rory had never seen so much money before in his life. He and his mum could buy their way out of Gloom with this!

For a moment, he thought to run home and tell her to pack her things because they'd be going away. But just as suddenly, the thought left his head. That would be stealing.

This was an advance of sorts, for a job he had yet to perform. Lord Foxglove trusted him for some strange reason. It was wrong to steal.

Rory stuffed the pouch in his pack and headed home, the coins clinking with every step he took.

CHAPTER SIX

Isabella, Also Known as Izzy

Rory walked home along the docks, the pouch of coins safe in his front pocket. He wanted to keep it close to his body, just in case he saw any villains about. His head was spinning. He and his mum would be able to pay off Bumbailiff for the rest of the year with this much money.

Suddenly, his mood darkened. What would he have to do to earn such a generous amount? Lord Foxglove said there were lots of duties to perform. But Rory could handle that. He knew how to do all kinds of things, and he had learned them all on his own. He knew how to tie a bowline and a reef knot, to scale and gut a fish in seconds, and to start a fire with wet leaves. He'd taken it upon himself to learn all these things through trial and error. He was curious like that.

Rory picked up his pace. A few men sat on the edge of one of the piers, passing a bottle between them. A frothy tide slapped against the pilings. Rory thought back to his interviews. The whole experience was extremely odd, Lord Foxglove being the oddest. Why was he so tall and thin? He looked like a skeleton. And were those teeth of his actually sharp, or was it just a strange trick of the dim light?

But the thing that concerned Rory most was that he'd have to live there. He'd never been away from home for more than a few hours, except for school, which didn't start again for another few months.

What would his mum do without him to run errands for her?

He had to take the job. Paying work was hard to come by in Gloom. He'd heard that lots of rich people were different. *Eccentric*, he thought it was called. That's what they were: eccentrics. That's all.

Rory was reminded of the tales people told about Foxglove Manor, which made him think about some of the other stories he'd heard over the years. Supposedly, people called mages went from town to town long ago, casting spells for those who could pay for their services. They healed sick sheep, filled dry wells with fresh water, and made barren fields bloom with seed.

Rory wasn't sure about all that. Just people making things up, he figured. But there was one story that everyone knew. It was the tale of Goldenrod, the Black Mariner. He was a sea captain who sailed the oceans of Europica. His hair was golden and his skin as black as the sea itself. He fought dragons that lived in the watery depths, tamed a giant seahorse as his steed, and once married a mermaid. Rory knew none of it could be real. But he liked the stories anyway.

As his home came into view, Rory ran the last few steps, flung open the door, and rushed inside, barely stopping to wipe his feet on the straw mat.

The house was warm, and the smell of shrimp stew filled the air. His mum sat at the kitchen table, scraping clams out of their shells with a small knife. Her red hair was loose and flowed down to the middle of her back. She looked up. Rory dropped the pouch, which landed on the table with a resounding *thunk*. Hilda Sorenson peered at the bag warily.

"Go on, then." Rory urged her. "Open it."

Hilda continued to stare. Finally, she picked up the pouch and shook it. The sound of clinking coins rang out.

"Is this what I think it is?" she asked, an air of wonder in her voice.

"Open it," Rory said again.

Hilda slowly loosened the drawstring and leaned her head forward. Her eyes grew as large as teacups. "All this?" she said in astonishment. "Is this . . . is this from the job? Why, you've barely even begun."

Rory smiled. "I know," he said. "I actually don't start until tomorrow. I had to meet Lord Foxglove first. Make it official and all that."

Hilda upturned the bag. Gleaming coins clattered onto the table, forming a mound of silver, gold, and copper. Rory even saw a few doubloons, a type of gold coin from the far side of the world.

His mum stared for a long moment. "By the sea gods," she finally murmured, running her fingers through the glittering bounty. "Tears of a fish."

The shrimp stew was delicious, and Rory attacked it eagerly. "I'll have to live there," he said, slurping the last bit of broth from his bowl. "I'm supposed to look after him, you know. Do his errands and such."

Hilda's soup spoon froze in front of her mouth.

"Mum?" Rory said.

Hilda set down her spoon. "Live there? Away from home? But . . . surely you'll have a day off now and then?"

Rory wasn't certain about that. Neither Lord Foxglove nor Malvonius had mentioned it. "I suppose so," he said. "I'm sure they'll tell me more when I start."

Hilda leaned back in her chair and sighed. "Your da would be so proud of you," she said, eyes shining, and then she sniffled, which made Rory's eyes water too.

He didn't know his father, and his mum didn't talk about him often. He had died before Rory was born. He was a sailor who'd drowned at sea, his mum had told him. Rory's only connection to him was the stone he wore around his neck —a misshapen nugget of black onyx threaded through with a silver chain. His mum said Rory's da had given it to her before he left on his fateful trip.

Rory fingered the chain as he thought of the father he never knew.

After supper, Rory made his way to Black Maddie's. He still had to tell Izzy about his new job and say goodbye. They wouldn't be seeing too much of each other if he was going to live at Foxglove Manor.

Live at Foxglove Manor.

The thought struck him like lightning. He was actually going to leave home. But his mum would be close, he consoled himself. It's not like he would be traveling across the globe, like Goldenrod did in his adventures.

It was early evening now, and the gas lamps sputtered and hissed, casting a sickly glow on the cobblestone streets. Rory walked briskly and kept his eyes and ears peeled. One of the gangs in Gloom was called the Canaries, and Rory didn't want to run into them. They wore pale yellow slickers and black wool caps that they pulled over their faces during getaways. People said they liked to make their victims *sing*. He wasn't exactly sure what that meant, and he didn't want to find out.

A slight rain began to fall, and Rory felt the fine drizzle on the back of his neck. He made his way up the Strasse until he got to Black Maddie's, then wiped his feet on the mat and stepped inside. Shouting from the barkeeps and mingled voices greeted him. He wound his way through the noisy patrons and toward a little room in the back. A thin red curtain served as a door. Candlelight flickered within. He pulled the curtain aside.

A girl the same age as Rory looked up from a table, a deck of painted wooden cards fanned out in front of her. Her hair was red and frizzy, with corkscrew curls going every which way. A spray of freckles peppered her face.

"There you are," Izzy said. "Where you been hiding?"

"Hey, Izzy," Rory greeted her. "No customers?"

"Been slow all night," she moaned, and plucked one of the cards with her forefinger.

Rory sat in the little chair reserved for patrons and looked at his friend. They'd known each other since they were small. They were neighbors and grew up together. Best of all, they shared a birthday, though for some reason, Rory couldn't remember the last time there was a birthday party in Gloom.

"I got a job," he said proudly.

"Where?" Izzy exclaimed. "At the docks? You're not old enough."

"No. Not the docks. It's . . . Guess."

Izzy rolled her eyes. "Oh, come on!" she complained, but Rory wouldn't budge. She twirled a strand of hair around her finger. "Chimney sweep?" she ventured.

"Nope."

"Lamplighter?"

"Nope."

"Bird poop sweeper?"

"Nope."

"Fish gutter?"

"Nope."

"Bird poop sweeper?"

"You already said that."

Izzy blew out a breath. "Okay. Enough, you urchin. What is it?"

Rory, now satisfied, leaned back in his chair and placed his thumbs behind imaginary suspenders. "I'm going to be a valet at Foxglove Manor."

Izzy wasn't easily frightened or impressed, but the look on her face was something between the two.

"The manor?" she said. "That creepy old place? Great seas, are you mad?"

"That's just a bunch of stories," Rory protested. "They already gave me an advance on my earnings. Mum can pay off Bumbailiff for a whole year!"

Izzy made a sour face at the mention of the landlord. Everyone on Copper Street knew him, and he was despised by them all.

"Interesting," she said. "So what's a valet do anyway?"

"I don't know," Rory confessed. "All kinds of stuff. I'll have to live there for a while too."

Izzy looked down at her cards and then back up again. "Our little Rory's come up in the world, hasn't he?" she teased. "Gonna forget about all your friends, then? You'll be working in the mansion, serving tea and biscuits to important folk."

Rory smiled. He knew his friend was only saying this because she was going to miss him.

Izzy drew the cards together so they formed a stack. "I'll have to read your fortune first. Can't go running off without knowing what you're getting into, right?"

"I guess so," Rory agreed.

A bottle shattered on the floor beyond the curtain, followed by shouting.

Izzy looked past Rory for a moment and then swept a strand of hair from her face. She pushed the deck in front of him. "Pick one."

Rory didn't really believe in Izzy's carved deck, but other people did. She wouldn't have a job at Black Maddie's reading fortunes if they didn't. He lifted a card from the deck.

"Scorpion," Izzy said, and placed it face-up at the table's edge. "Go again."

Rory drew another.

"Goat. One more."

Rory turned over the next card.

He sucked in a breath.

It was a hanged man, his neck cocked at a gruesome angle.

Izzy tapped her finger on the image. "Hmm," she murmured, and put the card next to the others. She studied them for a long moment.

"What does it mean?" Rory finally asked. He didn't want to seem frightened, so he kept his voice as steady as he could.

"Don't worry," Izzy replied. "It doesn't mean you're gonna get hanged. The hanged man means doubt. Uncertainty." She pushed the goat card forward. "But the goat represents you. And the scorpion is a threat."

Rory swallowed. He didn't understand how she could get all this from a bunch of painted wooden cards. Then again, Izzy's family was known for being a bit strange, even for a place like Gloom. She once told Rory that her mum came from a long line of witches, but he thought she was just having a laugh. Whenever he pressed her on it, she always turned the conversation to another subject.

"The scorpion's sting can kill the goat," Izzy said, bringing him back to the moment.

Rory shifted in the hard wooden seat. "What does it mean?" he asked again.

Izzy swept the cards back toward her. She stared at him. "It means you have to be careful, Rory. Very, very careful."

CHAPTER SEVEN

The Valet's First Day

As Rory tried to sleep that night, he thought more and more about what Izzy's cards had revealed. Even though he didn't believe in her fortune-telling, it still got under his skin.

He remembered a few of the strange things his best friend had done over the years, things he couldn't rightly explain. Once, when they were sitting on the docks of Quintus Harbor, Izzy called out to a bird, and to Rory's amazement, the black-and-white magpie landed on Izzy's hand, its small, glittering eyes blinking rapidly. Another time, when they were exploring the Glades, he could have sworn she started a campfire without flame or kindling.

Just coincidences, he told himself. *Or tricks of the eye.*

Rory rolled over in bed and sniffed the air. The pleasing aroma of fried clams and hot bread drifted up the stairs. His mum must have gotten up early just to make him a good meal. That didn't happen often. She usually slept late because she worked into the night at Black Maddie's.

He rose from his small bed and splashed water on his face from the basin on his nightstand. It was cold, but he didn't feel like heating it. He needed to get going.

He stuffed the few pairs of pants and shirts he owned into an old canvas bag, along with his best socks (the ones without holes), a deck of playing cards, and an assortment of rocks he'd been saving for as long as he could remember. He wasn't sure what he would do with the cards and the rocks, but he took them anyway. It was a comfort of sorts, to have a few mementos from home in his bag and pockets.

As for the advance Lord Foxglove had given him, Rory's mum would be paying a visit to the notorious Mr. Bumbailiff first thing that morning. Rory wished he could stick around long enough to see the expression on the awful man's face when the debt was paid off, but knowing he and his mum were in the clear was reward enough.

Rory looked in the small piece of mirror glass nailed to the wall. He dragged a comb through his curly hair. At one time, he'd thought about growing it out in long, ropy strands, a style he'd seen on a sailor who'd stopped in Gloom for a respite from the sea. The man had skin like him, dark and smooth. Rory had wanted to talk to the sailor to find out where he came from and where he was going. What had he seen in the great, wide world? Rory never gained the courage though, and only watched him from afar and made up stories about him.

His mother greeted him as he walked into the kitchen. "Thought you could do with a nice breakfast first," she said.

The coal stove was hot, and the room was cozy. Wan light trickled in through the one small window. The cries of birds sounded outside.

"Thanks, Mum," Rory replied, and sat down.

This was a special breakfast, Rory realized. He usually had a piece of fried bread or a boiled egg. It seemed his mum wanted to send him off with a full belly.

As Rory ate, he wondered how soon he'd be able to come back and visit. He imagined his mum was thinking the same thing, as she studied him intently, a forlorn look plain on her face.

He ate the last of the clams and then sopped up the sauce with his bread. His mum hugged him tight, and he inhaled the woodsy scent of patchouli oil. Every morning, she dropped a trembling bead of the liquid from a stopper onto her wrists and rubbed them together. "Do your best, Rory," she said. "I know you'll do a good job."

Rory knew he couldn't let her down. She was counting on him. He had to make her proud. "I will, Mum," he said.

And with that, he threw his bag over his shoulder and headed to Foxglove Manor.

Cool sea air caressed Rory's cheeks as he walked. He looked out over the bay and was reminded of the time that he and his friend Petru had spent an afternoon on the ocean. Petru's father had taken them out on his small, single-mast ship, but the trip was cut short when a storm suddenly hit. The boat rocked back and forth on the water, dipping and bobbing, sending seawater onto the deck and soaking Rory's clothes and face. He remembered the color of the sky that day. The clouds had been bruised and angry, almost completely black. But he hadn't been scared. He'd actually enjoyed it, and had wondered what it would be like to spend your life on the sea.

The loud cry of a gull snapped Rory out of his daydream. Now wasn't the time for lollygagging. Izzy's words came back to him again: *It means you have to be careful, Rory. Very, very careful.*

What exactly did that mean? he wondered. *Is something bad going to happen at Foxglove Manor?*

He shook the thought away and continued on. He didn't believe in Izzy's carved deck, anyway.

Rory spent the first day at Foxglove Manor learning all about the house. Malvonius led him around as if he were on a leash behind him, barking commands with brusque efficiency:

"Off-limits."

"Floors should be scrubbed every other day."

"Polish the brass doorknobs."

"Sweep the carpets."

And all manner of other duties. Outside, Malvonius had shown Rory a rambling tangle of weeds, plants, and shrubs that was supposed to be a garden. It would need tending as well. He certainly had his work cut out for him.

The right side of the main hall revealed a small powder room, which is where people went to wash up, Rory knew, even though he had never been in one. Beyond that was the drawing room—where he'd had his first interview. Farther down, the suit of armor stood guard before the right turn that led to the red door and Lord Foxglove's cellar study. To the left of the hall was another powder room, a kitchen, and something called the "great room," which had dramatic double doors and was for "very important guests," Rory was told.

"Where's Lord Foxglove's bedroom?" Rory asked.

Malvonius stopped and peered down at him. "The lord of the manor roams wherever he pleases. It is not the concern of servants."

Rory looked away, embarrassed. He really didn't like Malvonius Root. Not one bit.

Upstairs was a suite of dusty rooms, the smallest of which was situated at the end of a dim hall and was to be Rory's. The only source of light in the hallway came from a paraffin lamp set upon a long table shoved against the wall.

Rory's room was more like a closet, really. There was a small wooden bed and side table, a pitcher and basin for washing up, and a smelly oil lantern with a very short wick. The glass in the window over the bed was cracked. It was cold most nights, and the thin blanket did nothing to warm his bones. His meals, which were regular but not very appetizing

—mostly fish stew and bread—usually had to be eaten while sitting on the side of the bed with the plate on the low side table. Either that or balanced on his knees. Malvonius had said that he could eat in the kitchen only at the end of the day, as long as he didn't "disturb anyone," whatever that meant.

The manor not only had gas lamps but indoor plumbing as well. Unfortunately, Malvonius had told him the powder rooms were off-limits and reserved for guests. Rory had to make do with the basin in his room, which left a lot to be desired. If he wanted to clean with hot water, he had to fill a pot from the kitchen, heat it up on the stove, then carry the steaming kettle upstairs, all while trying to avoid the glare of Malvonius. Suffice it to say, he didn't bathe with hot water very often.

The odd thing was that even though Rory was hired as a valet, he never had much interaction with his employer. He kept Foxglove's coats and trousers clean with a boar-bristle brush that Malvonius had given him, but the lord of the manor kept to himself and never seemed to go anywhere. Rory didn't know why such care was taken for his master's appearance if he never entertained or even left the house.

Each morning, a note was tacked to Rory's door listing his duties. He supposed it was Malvonius who left them. The thin, spidery script seemed in keeping with the butler's mysterious demeanor. On any given day, Rory had to light and tend fireplaces, clean the mahogany furniture with water and lemon, sweep and beat the carpets, make sure the rooms were free of spiders and other creepy-crawlies, and, most important, polish Lord Foxglove's boots, which were made of leather so black Rory could see his reflection in them when he was finished.

One afternoon, Rory got a look at something he had been curious about ever since his first day, when Malvonius had showed him around the manor.

He was polishing the suit of armor at the end of the main hall when he heard the distinct clicking of Lord Foxglove's boots on the floor. Rory looked up as Malvonius and his employer strode past without so much as a glance and turned down the smaller hall to the right. Rory quickly peeked around the corner. They were standing in front of the red door.

Rory ducked back and ran the cloth along the armor, staying alert the whole while. He heard murmuring but not the actual words. It was much too dangerous to steal another glance.

There was a *click*, like a key being turned in a lock, and then a door being closed shut.

Rory stopped his polishing. He knew that the best way to do something dangerous was to do it right away, so he rushed around the corner.

He stepped up to the door. It was indeed red, but it was much more unusual than that.

A forest of black, spindly trees covered the entire surface, from top to bottom. He stared, and after a moment, it seemed as if the trees were swaying in an invisible breeze. Rory felt the hairs stand up at the back of his neck. The trees were definitely moving. He reached out with a hesitant hand, but stopped. A hissing sound came through the door, like the sound a bellows makes when it releases air.

Then footsteps on the other side.

Rory dashed back to the suit of armor, cloth in hand, and pretended to be obsessed with a spot of rust.

Lord Foxglove and Malvonius stepped out, none the wiser, and headed toward the cellar.

Rory breathed easier. He fingered the chain around his neck that held the black stone.

He didn't know what was behind the red door, but he was determined to find out.

CHAPTER EIGHT

A Feast Like No Other

Rory had slept uneasily the first few nights. He'd missed his mum—especially her cooking—and Izzy. He'd have to ask Malvonius if he was allowed a day off. He certainly couldn't be expected to work every day. Could he?

On his second week there, as Rory was polishing a silver candleholder, Malvonius seemed to appear out of thin air. "Tonight, Lord Foxglove will be having very special guests," Malvonius informed him. "You are to prepare the table and put out the linens. Do you understand?"

Rory looked up from his polishing and nodded. The butler's face was set in a permanent scowl, with frown lines so deep they looked like scars. Rory doubted the man had ever smiled. *How long has he been here?* he wondered. *Where did he meet Lord Foxglove? What is behind the red door?* So many unanswered questions.

As evening approached, Rory took out the fine, bone-white china from a cabinet and placed it around the table in the great room. Bronze and alabaster busts of important-looking people sat atop pedestals in each corner of the room.

Rory lit the candles on the table with a long matchstick, the reflected flames turning into soft pools of light in the dark surface of the tabletop. Malvonius watched him like a hawk as he worked. Rory then laid out the silverware—he knew exactly where each utensil should be placed because his mum had showed him how it was done one evening when her comrades came by for dinner. The meal had been a simple one of only clams, bread, and eel soup, but his mum had wanted things to be perfect.

Rory had no idea what Lord Foxglove's guests were going to eat. In fact, he had never even seen the kitchen staff or a cook. The only food he ever saw was the pot of meager fish stew bubbling on the stove every morning. It seemed to be made especially for him, as he never saw anyone else eating it.

The guests finally began to arrive later that evening. Malvonius answered the door, and Rory took coats, hats, and gloves in the main hall and hung them up in a closet. All of the invited guests looked at Rory curiously, like they were sizing him up for something. Rory committed each face to memory. It was a gift of his—once he saw a face, he never forgot it.

They came in every shape: tall, short, fat, and thin. Some had exquisite walking sticks. Others wore top hats. Some wore rings on their fingers. The women wore long dresses of red, gold, and black, their hair knotted up in elaborate designs. But what really stood out to Rory was their *scent*. It was a deep, earthy smell, musky and sharp.

Who are these people? he wondered. He'd never seen them around Gloom. They all had the same eyes as Lord Foxglove —pale and cold.

Rory hung up the last coat and turned at the sound of footsteps. Lord Foxglove came down the main hall, his boots clicking on the floor. "Lord Foxglove has arrived!" Malvonius announced.

There was a moment of reverent silence as the lord of the manor took in his guests. "Gentlemen," he finally said, pressing his hands together and looking around the hall. "Ladies. Are we ready to feast?"

Rory stood alone, unsure of what to do or where to go, as the guests rushed past him.

Malvonius pulled the double doors to the great room shut with a resounding thud.

Rory didn't understand.

What were they going to eat if there wasn't any food in there?

Rory pulled the ratty blanket more tightly around him. The bedroom was cold. He didn't even have a fireplace to keep warm. His thoughts drifted back to a few hours ago. Who were those strange guests? And what about the smell that clung to them, like a dog who had come in from the rain with damp fur? It was certainly a weird smell for a person to have.

He had stood outside the great room for what seemed an eternity, poised at attention and waiting for an order, but none ever came. All he had heard was a soft murmuring through the door every few minutes, but he couldn't make out any words. He yawned and shuffled his feet, then softly whistled a tune his mum had sung to him when he was little.

Finally, after two hours, he had gone upstairs. If he was supposed to stand sentry all night they should have told him, he reasoned. He wasn't going to linger there any longer doing nothing. So far, abandoning his post had not seemed to matter.

He turned over on his side. He couldn't sleep, although he was very tired and hungry. Before going to bed, he'd stolen into the empty kitchen and slurped some fish stew straight from the pot. He hadn't wanted to take a bowl upstairs because he'd just have to bring it back down again.

Rory turned over again. Muffled voices drifted through the floorboards. Every now and then, he thought he heard the tinkling of piano keys or the strumming of a harp, a sound he hadn't heard when he was downstairs. *Strange,* he thought. He'd never seen a real harp before, but his mum had something called a Victrola, and the lovely sounds of pianos, horns, and harps came out of it. It was a wonderous thing to hear, and he often sat in front of it for hours. It was like magic.

Rory sat up.

He had been awakened by a sound.

It was coming from downstairs. Where the guests were.

It was chanting. A chorus of low voices. There was no mistaking it. He threw off the thin blanket and knelt, putting his ear to the floor. For a moment all was silent, but then . . .

A shiver worked its way along his spine as a low growl seemed to come from downstairs. It was an animal sound, like a dog or a wolf. How was that possible?

He stood up and walked to the small window. Perhaps it was a stray animal outside. But he saw nothing of the sort, only the back garden of the manor, covered in high grass and weeds. He had to find out where the sound was coming from, but if he was caught, who knew what could happen?

He stared out the cracked window for a very long time. Cold air drifted through. *If I go searching,* he reasoned with himself, *and get caught, I'm done for.*

Then he wondered, *What would Izzy do?*

She'd take a chance, Rory knew. She was always up for doing things you weren't supposed to.

Rory released a sigh. He felt vibrations from the floor thrum along the soles of his bare feet. He took another deep breath, then walked to the door and opened it.

He slipped down the hallway as quiet as a mouse dressed in silk. He knew what he was doing could land him in hot water and possibly lose him his job, but he had to know what was making that sound. It was an itch that needed to be scratched.

The hallway was dark but for the paraffin lamp on the long table. He took the stairs on his tiptoes, every now and then pausing and holding his breath when a step groaned under his weight.

At the bottom, he walked into the hall, then snuck past the suit of armor, which stood guard silently. Rory thought it might come clattering to life and run him off with its lance at any moment.

He walked down the main hall. The doors to the great room were cracked open.

He had a decision to make. He could go in and look around or go back upstairs. Rory stood silently a moment, thinking, until his curiosity urged him on and he peeked around the doors.

The room was empty. And cold. Colder than it should have been. A smell hung in the air. It was the same odor he had noticed on the guests, like wet animal fur. He drew farther into the room.

And gasped.

The remains of several bones were on all of the plates. He bent down and looked more closely. The marrow had been sucked right out. He'd seen the bones that dogs had left behind and these looked very similar, chewed to bits and cracked open. "Tears of a fish," he whispered.

The low animal growl sounded once more and he followed it back out into the hall. All was quiet. He looked left, then right. There it was again—coming from farther away. He walked back the way he had come and passed the armor. Around the corner, a soft glow spilled along the floor. A floorboard creaked as he drew closer. He froze for a moment and sucked in a breath. The red door. The sounds were coming from behind it.

Rory moved silently, one step at a time. A red glow, as thin as a knife edge and deeper in color than the door itself, pulsed along its bottom. At first he thought it was firelight, but as he got closer, he realized that firelight wasn't really red. This was something else. Something . . . *unnatural.*

The red light continued to pulse, like it had its own heartbeat.

Strangest of all, the forest of black trees painted on the door seemed to be moving again, thin branches swaying silently.

He put his ear a few inches from the door and cupped it with his right hand. He almost expected to feel a tickling sensation from the phantom breeze, but to his relief, he felt no such thing. The low animal sound faded but was replaced by something even more mysterious:

Words.

"She is coming. I can feel her upon the wind."

"We will need more. Much more."

"Do not fret. A great harvest is coming."

And then, Rory heard a phrase he had never heard before:

"Long live Arcanus Creatura!"

Shuffling steps sounded behind him. He turned, his breath catching in his throat.

It was Malvonius.

CHAPTER NINE

The Valet Is Interrogated

Rory froze.

He couldn't move, even if he had wanted to. The blood felt cold in his veins.

Malvonius was still dressed in his butler's uniform. Did he ever sleep? Rory didn't even know where his room was.

His mismatched eyes glittered. "What are you doing?" he asked in his slow, deep voice.

It was a simple question, but Rory found himself at a loss for words. His tongue felt thick in his throat. "I, um . . . I thought I heard voices, and well . . . I came to see if someone was at the door."

Malvonius breathed out through his nostrils. "This is *not* the front door," he replied, like he was talking to a very small child. "That is around the corner." He pointed his long arm.

Rory's legs felt like sticks ready to break under his weight. He absently reached up and caressed the black stone around his neck. Malvonius was calm, but in that calmness, Rory sensed a deep, simmering anger, as if at any moment the butler could reach out and throttle him.

"What did you hear?" he asked, drawing closer.

"Nothing," Rory said, backing up a pace. "I heard nothing at all." But he knew the beads of sweat trembling on his forehead told another story.

Malvonius pinned him with those strange eyes of his. They didn't seem human. They were more like an animal's eyes. "Wandering about the house without permission can lead to . . . unfortunate events," he said in a low voice. "Now, I ask you again. What . . . did . . . you . . . *hear?*"

Rory swallowed loudly. "Nothing," he said. "I wasn't snooping."

Malvonius drew in a deep breath and then released it. "Lies," he hissed, drawing out the word.

And then Malvonius smiled, and it was full of malice.

"I'll see that the master hears of this," the butler said. "Oh yes. And then we shall see, won't we?"

Rory sat on his bed, hugging his knees to his chest. *Bones,* he thought with horror. What kind of bones were they? He couldn't tell, as they'd been ripped apart. Where did they come from?

He was terrified. What had he just done? He'd be let go, he realized. As soon as Lord Foxglove heard what happened, he'd have to leave immediately. He'd told his mum he was going to do a good job. And he had failed.

Rory didn't remember falling asleep, but he awoke to the sound of birds outside his window. For a moment he thought he was at home, snug in bed, but then the strangeness of the night before came flooding back.

She is coming. I can feel her upon the wind.

We will need more. Much more.

Do not fret. A great harvest is coming.

Long live Arcanus Creatura!

What does it all mean? Rory wondered. *What is Arcanus Creatura? Who is* she?

Rory dressed and began his day's duties hesitantly, constantly looking over his shoulder, waiting for Lord Foxglove to call him into that cold, dark cellar.

I'll see that the master hears of this.

He worked all morning—polishing the silverware, scrubbing the floors, and beating the dust out of the rugs with a *mattenklopper*, which made his eyes water and his throat itch.

His thoughts kept turning to Izzy and his mum. It felt like it had already been months since he had seen them.

As he ran a cloth over an already-gleaming table in the main hall, Malvonius came out of the drawing room.

"You have been summoned," he said.

"Summoned?" Rory echoed.

"Yes, *summoned*," Malvonius said with an edge. "The master will see you now. Put down that rag! This instant!"

Rory jumped where he stood and stuffed the cloth in his back pocket.

"Follow me," the butler commanded him.

Down the stairs they went, and Rory felt the familiar cold and damp. His legs trembled with each step he took. What kind of trouble was he going to get into? Izzy had warned him to be careful, but he was too curious. He just couldn't help himself.

A minute later, he was standing before Lord Foxglove. Malvonius retreated to the back of the room, lost in shadow, but Rory still felt his presence.

Foxglove sat at his desk, putting the finishing touches on a letter. Rory watched as he used candlewax to seal the envelope. He seemed to let the moment stretch out as long as possible, making Rory more uncomfortable with every passing second.

Finally, without looking up from his task, he said, "I understand you were out and about last evening."

Rory didn't know what to say. It wasn't really a question. But it was something he had to answer. "I . . . well, I heard voices and thought that maybe someone was at the door."

Lord Foxglove finally looked up. His pale eyes sent a chill right through Rory. He stood and came from around the table, oddly graceful despite his height and thin frame. "When you took this job," he began, "I believe you said you could be trusted. Is that not correct?"

Rory didn't remember being asked that. But maybe he had. It was as if he'd been in a daze the day he was hired.

"I gave you a very large sum to keep my trust and to perform your duties," the lord of the manor continued. "I don't give out money like that willy-nilly. Do you understand?"

"Yes, Mr. Fox—"

Malvonius coughed in the shadows.

"*Lord* Foxglove," Rory corrected himself.

Rory felt small standing in the tall man's presence. He wanted nothing more than to disappear. Foxglove bent down a little closer to Rory's face. His nose was sharp and long, and the beard he wore was braided into three strands, each as thick as a length of rope. Rory wanted to tie them into a knot and then yank as hard as he could.

Lord Foxglove reached out and lifted Rory's chin, and Rory flinched at his touch. "I think you are a very bright boy, but I do believe you are a curious sort. Is that not correct?"

Rory didn't like the way Lord Foxglove spoke to him, like he was trying to trick him with words. He also didn't like being held by the chin, but he was too scared to back away.

Foxglove didn't wait for an answer. "What did you hear?" he asked, releasing Rory and rising back up to his full height.

"I didn't hear anything," Rory said defiantly.

Lord Foxglove was silent for a long moment. The air in the room was so cold Rory wanted to wrap his arms around himself. Finally, Foxglove stepped back a pace. He clasped his hands together and spoke very quickly. "If I find you in a part of the house where you are not expected again, I'm afraid our little arrangement will come to an end."

Rory glanced at the black-and-white marble floor and then back to Lord Foxglove, although he didn't meet his eyes. *Is that it?* he wondered. A small sense of relief flooded through him. He wasn't going to be let go! He and his mum would still be okay.

His employer turned around and walked back to his desk. "Malvonius, escort young Rory to his room."

Malvonius slinked out of the shadows and pinched Rory's arm, leading him away.

CHAPTER TEN

A Glimpse, Nothing More

Rory had been awake since dawn.

Hunger gnawed at his stomach, made worse by the absence of his mum and Izzy. Before he'd started at the manor, he'd seen both of them nearly every day of his life. They were a constant source of support and friendship, and he missed them dearly. But he couldn't ask for a day off now, not after he'd nearly lost his job. He shifted his weight on the bed. Maybe he should just leave. He didn't like the manor, and it was probably only going to get worse.

Rory spent the next several days doing his chores as directed by the notes tacked to his door. He swept the same rooms over and over, dusted and mopped, and made sure to steer clear of the red door. Since the night he'd been caught eavesdropping, he'd heard nothing from within the mysterious room.

Long live Arcanus Creatura!

He pictured the door in his mind, and the way the thin tree branches painted onto it seemed to have been moving. *What could cause that to happen?*

She is coming. I can feel her upon the wind.

Who?

He shook the dark thoughts away. Whatever was going on behind the red door was none of his business. If he wanted to keep his job, he had to put snooping behind him.

One late afternoon at the end of the week, after Rory had cleaned, polished, swept, and mopped what seemed like every room in the manor, he found Malvonius shuffling through some papers at a desk in the drawing room. Rory approached him rather quietly, perhaps too much so.

"Excuse me, sir?" Rory said.

Malvonius jumped in his seat, startled.

Rory gasped.

For a brief second, he thought he saw — *knew* he saw — something else.

Something that was *not* Malvonius Root.

The butler had a different face — a wild, animal face with birdlike features that disappeared as soon as Rory blinked.

"Yes?" Malvonius asked, regaining his composure, completely unaware, it seemed, of what Rory thought he'd just seen.

Rory swallowed. "I, um . . . well . . ."

"Spit it out, boy, for goodness' sake!"

Rory shuddered. "We never talked about my day off, sir," he started. "I'd like to see my mum. Maybe this evening? I've finished all my duties, sir."

Malvonius leaned back in his chair and studied him. He looked down his long nose. "A day off? What's that?"

"It's, you know, when—"

"I know good and well what a day off is!" Malvonius cut him off. "But I've never found the need for one myself."

Rory wanted to punch him right in his smug face.

Malvonius thrust out his chin. "And you ask this *after* being caught gallivanting around the house at all hours?"

"I wasn't gallivanting."

Malvonius raised an eyebrow.

Rory shrunk.

"Perhaps he doesn't want the evening off after all," the

butler said in his menacing, quiet tone. "Perhaps he wants to work in the back garden, pulling weeds and chopping brambles."

"No!" Rory blurted out, and then immediately regretted it and lowered his voice. "I mean, I just need a little time, sir. See, my mum lives on her lonesome and all, and . . ."

Malvonius waved his hand as if shooing a fly. He fished a pocket watch from somewhere within his suit and looked at it closely. "Be back at half-past nine, no later," he declared. "If you're late, the master will hear of it." He clicked the watch shut. "Do you understand?"

Rory nodded.

There was a moment of silence.

"Is that quite all?" Malvonius asked, as if offended.

"Oh," Rory said. "Thank you, sir. Thank you very much."

"Humph." Malvonius sniffed, then lowered his head and went back to his work.

Rory turned around and headed out of the room. He swallowed a grin.

No matter how much Malvonius tormented him, it didn't matter. He was going to see his mum and Izzy again.

Hooray! he wanted to shout.

But he didn't.

Rory shut the door to Foxglove Manor and set off, resisting the urge to skip down the road. That was for kids. But he was happy. Happier than he'd been in days. He was going to see the two most important people in his life, and he couldn't wait.

He looked left, then right, and went ahead and skipped anyway, smiling the whole while.

He decided to pay a quick visit to Izzy first before going home. He had so much to tell her and he couldn't wait. He felt a little guilty for not seeing his mum first—if she was even home and not at work—but she'd want him to stay the whole time, and he definitely wanted to see his best friend before going back to that dreadful manor.

As he walked, happy to be free for even a short while, he wondered what, exactly, he had seen when he'd surprised Malvonius.

Maybe it really was just a trick of the eye, Rory told himself. After all, he was tired and stressed from all of the work and the thoughts of home swirling in his head. Whatever it was, it had sent a shiver right through him.

He made his way up the Strasse and turned onto Copper Street. The clouds above Gloom were even darker than usual. There was something strange in the air, he noticed, but he couldn't put his finger on it. Still, the familiarity of the neighborhood put him at ease—from the sharp tang of the leatherworks to the coppery smell of the iron foundry.

Izzy's house was just a half block down from his own, and he was there in a few minutes.

The door opened with a creak after he knocked.

"Rory?"

Izzy's mum, Pekka, stood before him. She was a tall woman with hair as curly as her daughter's. She held a small bowl and muddler in her hands. An earthy smell rose from the bowl. "Heard you're up at the manor now, eh?" she said, grinding whatever it was with the muddler. "Making a little money on your own, then?"

"Yes," Rory said, "for me and Mum."

"Rory!" Izzy shouted.

She rushed past her mum and threw her arms around him. Pekka jumped out of the way, almost dropping her bowl. "I thought you'd never show up again," Izzy said. "They got you locked in up there or sumthin'?"

Rory untangled himself, feeling a little embarrassed. They were best friends, but never really hugged each other. "I, um—"

But that's all he had time to say, as Izzy grabbed his hand and pulled him away.

"Be back for dinner!" Pekka shouted to their retreating backs.

Rory and Izzy had another favorite place to visit besides the docks at Quintus Harbor and the Glades. The Narcisse River ran parallel to the Strasse and was really more like a creek. The water was green and brackish, with several dead tree limbs rising above the surface, as if trying to reach the weak light of the seldom-seen sun. Birds chirped in the surrounding trees. Rory and Izzy sat on the bank, which was covered in soft green moss. Rory told her everything that had happened at Foxglove Manor. "It's odd," he said. "The whole place is strange."

"But you can leave though, right?" Izzy asked. "No one's keeping you prisoner."

Rory shook his head and fiddled with a broken twig. "We need the money, Izzy. It's just me and Mum. You know that."

The deep rumbling of a toad sounded through the swampy reeds below. "Tell me what you heard again," Izzy demanded. "The words through the door."

The strange phrases came back to Rory easily. He didn't think he'd ever forget them. "I heard, 'She is coming. I can feel her upon the wind.' And, 'Long live Arcanus Creatura.'"

Izzy nodded. "And the other words?"

"'A great harvest is coming. We will need more. Much more.'" The words gave him a vague sense of unease in the pit of his stomach.

"That *is* strange," Izzy murmured.

"Do you know what any of it means?"

Izzy twirled a corkscrew curl around one finger. A moment of silence hung between them. "You know the cards I use? You know what they do, right?"

"Yeah," Rory replied. "They tell people's fortunes."

"Right, but it's a system — the minor and major . . . *arcana*."

Rory's ears twitched. "Arcana? Is that the same as arcanus?"

"Yes. Arcana means secret or mystery."

"And creatura?"

"I don't know that one. But it sounds like . . . *creature*."

Rory tensed. "Secret . . . *creature?*"

Izzy nodded.

The vision of Malvonius and the animal face flashed in Rory's mind. He swallowed. "Before I left today, I walked up on Malvonius, and he didn't see me coming. I surprised him, and for a second, he looked . . . odd."

"Odd?" Izzy repeated. "Of course he's odd. You already told me that."

"I mean *really* odd." Rory persisted. "His face. It was like, for a second, I thought I was looking at an animal face. I know it sounds crazy."

Izzy's brow wrinkled in concern. "An animal?"

Rory tried to conjure up the memory. "It happened so fast I can barely remember. It was like a bird of some sort, with sharp eyes. It just kind of shimmered and then disappeared."

Rory relaxed his shoulders. Just telling the story had made him tense. A fly landed on his neck, and he swatted it away. A fishy smell rose off the river.

Izzy turned away from the water to face him. "Remember what I told you? When I read your cards?"

He did, but he didn't answer. The air was cool on his face.

"The cards said to be careful."

Rory looked past the water, into the bare trees on the other side. A yellow-eyed hawk sat on a limb, patiently waiting for prey.

"Bones," Izzy continued. "Animal faces. Strange words from a locked room. Sounds like a mystery."

"What should I do?" Rory asked.

"Don't do anything right now," Izzy replied. "Watch and learn. And if anything else weird happens, we'll go from there."

Rory nodded in agreement, but he didn't want anything else weird to happen. He just wanted things to be normal. He turned to Izzy. "We?" he said.

Izzy smirked. "Of course, you urchin. You're not getting involved in some adventure without me."

Rory smiled despite the ball of fear beginning to form in his stomach.

CHAPTER ELEVEN

An Evening in the Salon

Rory saw Izzy home. They stood outside her door for a moment. A breeze stirred the air around them.

"Be careful, Rory," she said again. "If you find anything out, you gotta let me know. Okay?"

Rory looked at his friend. "I will," he said, "but it might be hard to get out again. I promise to try."

"You better," Izzy warned him. "You don't want to see me angry."

He gulped, then smiled, wanting to leave her on a good note. He knew she was kidding, even though her eyes flashed strangely for a moment before she went inside.

Rory turned and walked toward home. The time was passing too quickly. He only had a few hours left. The sky was dark already.

He opened the door to his house.

"Rory!" His mum rushed over and drew him into her arms. Thoughts of Foxglove and Malvonius left him immediately as the familiar scent of patchouli rose in his nostrils. His heart swelled. He'd missed her. More than anything.

"Ah, there he is," said Ox Bells. "The young master returns."

Rory looked past his mum to find that their small sitting room was filled with her comrades: Vincent, Ox Bells, and Miss Cora. He could see that some of the money Foxglove had given him had already been put to good use. There was a new couch and the walls had a fresh coat of red paint.

Rory stepped farther inside their front room, "the salon" as his mum called it. A few apples, a bottle of wine, and dried nuts had been placed on the table. Rory immediately reached for the nuts and popped a few in his mouth. Ox Bells clapped him on the shoulder—hard—which made Rory wince.

"What's everyone doing here?" he asked.

"Just one of our little gatherings," his mum said. "Cora shared a new poem with us earlier."

Rory took a seat on the couch, and his mum joined him.

The others were seated upon the few threadbare chairs spread around the room. Miss Cora, who was in the chair closest to Rory, waved her hand in the air dramatically. "I call it 'The Journey of the Silver Faun,'" she said.

Rory didn't know what a faun was and was about to ask, but Vincent spoke first. "Tell us all about your adventure at the manor," he demanded, his monocle glinting in his left eye. His cane was propped against the chair he sat in.

"Yes," chimed in Cora, caressing a feather boa coiled around her neck. "What's *really* going on in that dreadful house? Ghosts? Spirits?"

Rory swallowed. Could he tell them? What would they think? Would his mum tell him to leave the manor immediately?

She shot him a concerned glance. Rory remembered she'd seemed a little hesitant when he'd first told her about the job. "You haven't seen anything strange there, have you, Rory?"

Now's the time, Rory thought. His mum's friends had lived in Gloom forever. Maybe they knew something about Arcanus Creatura or the other strange phrases.

"No," he said instead. "Just a dusty, old house."

Vincent looked at Rory skeptically. "Years ago, I knew a man who said that Foxglove Manor was full of spirits. He said he saw one himself while attending a ball."

"Ball?" questioned Hilda. "What kind of ball?"

Vincent withdrew a silk cloth from his breast pocket, then removed his monocle from his eye and polished it. "An affair, darling," he explained. "A grand affair with important guests from far away. There was music, dancing, *and*—my friend said—a secret ritual at the stroke of midnight." He replaced the glass eyepiece.

Miss Cora and Ox Bells sat motionless, enthralled by Vincent's tale.

Rory's pulse raced. "What . . . kind of ritual?"

Vincent looked at each of them for a long moment, clearly relishing the attention. "Well," he continued, lowering his voice, "my friend said it was all about summoning a priestess. One from the old world."

There was a moment of silence.

"Tears of a fish," Rory's mum said with a dismissive wave of her hand. "I've heard enough. Don't need you putting stories in my Rory's head." She gave Rory a sympathetic look, like he was a child who needed to be protected.

Ox Bells took a bite of an apple, splitting it clean in half with one great chomp, and began to talk with his mouth full. "Years ago, when I was in the circus, the ringmaster said he wouldn't come to Gloom because of Foxglove Manor. Said something dark was in there. Something . . . evil." He took another huge bite, chewed loudly, swallowed, and then belched. "Any more apples, Hilda?"

Rory's mum ignored him. "Don't you believe him, Rory. He's mad, I tell you. Bloomin' mad."

Rory forced a smile, but the animal face he'd seen on Malvonius and the words he'd heard behind the red door were heavy on his mind.

A priestess from the old world, Vincent had just said.

She is coming. I can feel her upon the wind.

Could Foxglove's strange guests have been talking about a priestess? Rory wondered.

Hilda heated up fish stew on the stove and then passed bowls around the table. Even though fish stew was all Rory had eaten at the manor, his mum's recipe put that gruel to shame. He leaned his head down and inhaled deeply. A mélange of seasonings wafted toward his nose: basil and marjoram and pepper. It was a smell he'd desperately missed.

"Don't they feed you in that place?" Miss Cora asked, watching Rory sop up his stew with a heel of bread.

Rory didn't look up from his bowl. "Not much," he said.

"Nothing like home cooking," Ox Bells said, patting his expansive stomach.

"Yes," Rory's mum said. "You should try it sometime."

"And why would I do that, Hilda," Ox Bells replied, "when you set such a fine table yourself?"

Vincent laughed so hard he almost lost his monocle.

Rory looked around the table and smiled. He was glad his mum had good friends to keep her company while he was away.

After they were finished and the plates and bowls were put away, everyone drank small glasses of wine, except for Rory, who settled on a mug of tea.

"Who's up for a tale, then?" Vincent asked. Rory knew Vincent was the storyteller of the group and had heard a few of his tales himself, usually outlandish ones. They all nodded, and Vincent shifted in his seat.

"Many years ago," he began, "there lived a very bright boy who loved the sea. His mother was a great sailor, who was known for her daring voyages to unknown waters."

"His *mother*?" Cora asked.

"Indeed," Vincent replied, "she was of Sumerian blood, and the women of that noble lineage were renowned adventurers."

Rory's ears pricked up. He'd heard of the Sumerians. They were an ancient people recognized by their dark skin and skill on the water. But he'd been told they were long gone now, lost in the ebb and flow of history.

"Now, this boy liked to sail very much," continued

Vincent, "and was always asking his mother about her adventures, but she forbade him from going too far out on the water himself without her accompaniment, lest he be lost.

"But one evening, he began building a boat in secret, while the people of the village slept. He used the finest ash and pine to build the hull, polished the deck with myrrh and lavender oil. The finishing touch was the prow—a mermaid sculpted from red lapis."

"Lapis?" Miss Cora whispered. "The rarest of gemstones."

"Indeed," Vincent replied. "The rarest in the world, found only in the great mines of Sumer." He lifted his wine glass and took a long swallow. Rory sat silently, drawn into the story. He could see the boat as Vincent had described it, polished wood gleaming in the sun. How he longed to sail himself one day.

"Finally, the time came," Vincent continued, setting his glass back down. "The boy had finished his work. When he took the ship out, it glided on the water like no other vessel before it. He sailed to the far edge of the continent, where, under the diamond stars, he learned the mysteries of the sea mages."

"Sea mages?" Rory whispered. He had heard of mages before, but not these. "Who are they?" he asked.

"*Were*," Vincent corrected him, "for they no longer roam

this earth. But they were men and women with great knowledge, Rory. Some said they could read the thoughts of others and have them do their bidding, that they tamed creatures from the depths of the ocean and used them as their steeds, and that they could quiet raging storms by casting spells."

Rory saw images of Vincent's tale in his head as he spoke. "Goldenrod," he said. "The boy you're talking about grew up to become Goldenrod, the Black Mariner."

Vincent ran his fingers across his ivory-tipped cane. "The one and only," he replied.

"Goldenrod is a myth," Hilda scoffed. "A children's story."

Rory wasn't sure whether he believed in Goldenrod or not. He knew it was probably like his mum said: tales of Goldenrod were for children, stories meant to plant a spark of imagination in the otherwise dull lives of Gloom's citizens.

But still . . .

"He's just a man," Ox Bells suddenly declared. "Nothing more."

"They say he's fighting a war on the far side of the world," Miss Cora added.

"War?" Ox Bells scoffed. "If there were a war, I'd know about it."

Hilda smirked. "Oh really?"

Ox Bells puffed out his already large chest. "I've fought with the best of them," he boasted. "Brigands, pirates, smugglers."

"Those were *bar* fights," Vincent said. "The war Cora speaks of is real." He paused, basking in the moment again. "It is an *invisible* war, fought in the shadows."

The air in the room suddenly felt very close. Rory tugged at his collar and absently touched the black stone around his neck. "Invisible?" he heard himself ask.

"How can a war be invisible?" his mum added.

"It is beyond our understanding," Vincent said. "But a great war is being waged out in the larger world. I've heard stories of flames in the clouds and vengeful spirits riding the wind."

"And where have you heard this?" Cora asked. Her eyes were heavy lidded. Perhaps she'd had too much wine, Rory mused.

Vincent sniffed. "I have my sources. Believe it or not, there is much more to the world than this sad, little town."

There was a moment of silence.

Could it be true? Rory wondered. *A great war being fought that no one in Gloom even knew about?*

"Well," Hilda said, "the only war I know about is the battle to get fresh vegetables around here."

Laughter broke the ominous atmosphere. A night bird whistled outside. Rory yawned. He was getting tired and knew that, soon, he'd have to leave the comfort of his home behind and head back to the manor. The thought filled him with dread. He didn't want to go. It was warm and cozy here, and his belly was full.

"Who's up for a song, then?" Hilda asked.

They all murmured in agreement, and as Rory watched and listened, his mum began to sing a song about a mermaid trapped on land and longing for the sea.

CHAPTER TWELVE

Portraits in the Hall

Rory returned to Foxglove Manor just before nine, tiptoed up the stairs, and slipped into his room. The house was quiet, and he saw no sign of Malvonius or Foxglove. *Probably down in that cold cellar,* Rory thought. *Or in the room with the red door.*

Do not fret. A great harvest is coming.

He thought of what Vincent had said earlier that evening: *. . . summoning a priestess. One from the old world.*

Something dark was in there, Ox Bells had added. *Something . . . evil.*

Was it real or just stories? Maybe he should have asked his

mum's comrades about Arcanus Creatura after all. Vincent sure seemed to know a lot about Foxglove Manor and other mysterious things. But then his mum would worry about him, and that was the last thing Rory wanted her to do.

He got into bed and stared up at the ceiling. He felt the weight of the house settling over him, like he was being smothered. He wished more than anything that he was back home in his own familiar room. He felt safe and loved there, not like here, where he seemed to be more of a nuisance to his employers than a help.

He soon fell into an uneasy asleep, thoughts of Goldenrod and the invisible war flickering in his mind.

Rory didn't receive a note in the morning instructing him on the day's duties, but that didn't mean there wouldn't be any work. Malvonius cornered him in the hall when Rory came downstairs. "You must polish all of the frames in the main hall," the butler instructed him. "They hold very valuable paintings. If you damage any of them, even the slightest scratch, it will be at a great cost to you. Do you understand?"

"Yes," Rory said immediately. He didn't want to give Malvonius the slightest reason to admonish him, so he kept his head down and his answers short. He thought of the animal face again. What was it? *Creatura*. Creature, Izzy had said.

Malvonius set down a bucket at Rory's feet. "Use this," he barked. "You'll find brushes, rags, and a cleaning solution."

Rory picked up the bucket.

"Remember," Malvonius said. "Do not damage the paintings."

Rory nodded, then took the bucket and walked down the hall toward the front door. His stomach rumbled. Even though he hated the fish stew, he needed something in his belly, but it didn't look like it was going to happen. He set the bucket on the floor and took out one of the smelly rags, then poured a little of the solution onto it. The fumes made his eyes water. He held his breath as he began to carefully clean the nooks and crannies of an ornate gold leaf frame. It held a portrait of what must have been Lord Foxglove in his younger days. The man had the same cruel eyes as Rory's employer. His head was still bald, but he had no beard, revealing a bratty expression on his smug face. He was standing before a fountain, with one hand on his hip and the other up in the air, as if giving a speech. Rory snickered. Foxglove sure was full of himself. Rory used a fine brush to get into the intricate corners of the frame, which were molded in the shape of rose petals.

He worked carefully, but absently, with thoughts of home and Izzy foremost on his mind. He really didn't like it here. But he and his mum had money, and that was the most important thing. She had seemed so happy the night before. He couldn't just leave his job. He wondered how much of the money his mum had given Mr. Bumbailiff—hopefully enough for a few months, at least.

Rory stood back and studied his cleaning. One smudge in the bottom right of the gold frame made him reach in with a clean cloth to polish it, and when he did, he saw the artist's signature, written in a tiny, cramped script, along with a location: *Lysander Swoop. Captain's Quay.*

"Humph," Rory muttered. He'd heard of Captain's Quay. It was a neighborhood on the other side of town, to the west of Copper Street and Market Square.

He moved on to the next frame, a large brass circle. The painting inside it showed a woman with hair as long as seagrass and eyes the color of green gemstones. Rory looked along the portrait's bottom edge. There it was again: *Lysander Swoop. Captain's Quay.*

He checked the next painting—a man on horseback, his hair blowing in the wind: *Lysander Swoop. Captain's Quay.*

And next to that one, a woman who looked as if she had just smelled something really bad, her lips curled in a grimace: *Lysander Swoop. Captain's Quay.*

All the faces were familiar, he realized with a start. Even

though they were younger, they were certainly some of Fox-glove's guests from the night Rory had heard the mysterious words behind the red door.

He stepped back and looked down the long hall. Were all of the paintings done by this man, Lysander Swoop? And how long ago had he painted them? *Maybe if I find him,* Rory thought, *he can tell me something about Foxglove.* Perhaps he would know what "a great harvest is coming" meant.

No, Rory told himself.

Snooping was forbidden. If he got in trouble again, he would definitely be dismissed.

He stared at the painting of Foxglove and thought for a moment.

Who says I can't look for Lysander Swoop? he asked himself. *What I do outside the manor is my own business.* Izzy would tell him to do it. They had to find out what the mysterious words meant and what Foxglove and his guests were doing behind the red door. It could be something important.

Something dark was in there. Something . . . evil.

A plan began to take shape in Rory's mind. All he had to do was find a way to get out again, so he and Izzy could search for Lysander Swoop.

He paused. *Find a way to get out again.*

Was he a prisoner, like Izzy had said?

Of course not. He could leave anytime he wanted to. He could throw down his smelly rag right now and tell Foxglove to do his own dirty work.

Except . . .

He couldn't.

The advance on his earnings was a way to make sure he didn't go running off after a day or two. People in Gloom were honest—at least most of them.

He continued to polish the frames, the sharp odor of the cleaning fluid burning his nostrils. Finally, after several hours, he was finished. Sweat dotted his brow. The rumbling in his stomach was now a tight, churning ball. He had to eat something. Anything.

Rory set down the cleaning tools and walked into the kitchen. He hoped to find a heel of bread on the table but was disappointed to see only the usual pot on the stove. He opened the lid. A thin layer of oil or . . . *something* floated on the surface of the fish stew.

Rory swallowed a gag, but his belly was empty. He needed to fill it. Reluctantly, he set the lid aside and picked up the wooden spoon beside the pot, then skimmed some of the grease away to get a spoonful of the fish. He brought it to his mouth and slurped some down. Pushing his revulsion to the back of his mind, he did it again. And again. He filled a tin cup with water and drank it eagerly, trying to wash away the terrible taste.

The pain in his stomach slowly disappeared as he sat at the table. He let out a breath and wondered what he should be doing next. He didn't want to get caught lollygagging but didn't want to roam around the house without a purpose either.

He rose from the table and set about washing his glass. He looked out the window at the back garden. A tiny patch of sun filtered through some of the trees. He didn't see sun in Gloom often, and more than anything, he wanted to run outside and feel the warmth on his skin.

Hmm, he thought to himself, noticing the tall weeds. *I'll go outside and do some work in the back garden. That'll show some self-motivation. Plus, I'll get a little sun.*

Rory rinsed out the glass and set it on the counter.

It was less of a garden and more of a jungle, with thorny shrubs, creeping vines, and all manner of weeds. He found a spade and a pair of rusty shears in a bucket and got to work. There was a small patch of garden at home, and he and his mum worked together in the warm months tending to the soil, trying to make things grow. Unfortunately, the dim sunlight made it a difficult task. But weeds and ivy didn't need a lot of sun to thrive.

Rory knelt next to a tangle of brambles and started cutting. It was hard work, and even though the air was cool, the weak sun felt good on the back of his neck.

He chopped at a thick, gnarled root with the spade and began to hum a tune. It was a song his mum used to sing to him when he was young, and the melody came back easily.

The Dragon of the Sea,
a mighty sailor was he.
But his ship was lost . . .

Thunk.

Rory stopped his digging. He had hit something hard. *A stone?*

He tapped the point of the spade into the ground.

Thunk. Thunk.

There was definitely something there. He could feel it.

He dug around until he saw a black square about the size of one of Izzy's cards. He looked back toward the house and its windows. No sign of Malvonius.

Rory set down the spade and carefully brushed away the dirt with his hand. It was a box. It looked like it could have been lacquered at one time; some of the sheen was still visible. He lifted it from the ground. A silver hinge fastened it shut. Rory unclasped it. He lifted the lid.

Inside the box was a heart.

CHAPTER THIRTEEN

A Lacquered Box and
What He Found Within

Rory knew what it was.

There was no mistaking it. He had seen a cow's heart once at the butcher's stall when his mum had asked him to get some meat for supper. The butcher, a big man named Henry, told him it was a delicacy, something fancy people liked to eat with rosemary and capers. There certainly couldn't've been much difference between an animal and a human heart.

Who would bury a human heart?

Foxglove would, Rory realized. Even though he had no idea why.

He stared at it again.

Maybe it wasn't human, he suddenly considered. It could be an animal of some sort.

Rory released a trembling breath.

He didn't know what to do.

Rebury it?

Show it to his mum and her comrades?

But how was he going to get a day off again so quickly?

He glanced back toward the house. Dark clouds were rolling in. A drop of rain landed on his head. He closed the lid and, with one last look at the house, lifted his shirt and tucked the box halfway into the waistband of his pants, letting his shirttail cover the rest of it.

Rory made it to his room without any sign of Malvonius. He was glad of it. After a few steps, the box had begun to slip, and he'd had to take it out and rush inside and close the door.

He slid the box under his bed, then stood in front of the little basin and washed the dirt from his hands and face. He watched the grime sluice off him, turning the water black.

He raised his head.

It was a heart, he thought with revulsion, understanding just how truly strange it was. *A human heart.*

There were still a few hours left in the workday, so after

washing up, he went back down and swept the already-clean floors. He had to make things appear normal, even though they were far from it. He didn't want to make Malvonius suspicious.

Later, he sat on the edge of the bed, exhausted. *Whose heart is it?* he wondered.

They weren't getting it back, that was certain. Whomever it belonged to was dead. Someone had killed him. *Or her,* Rory realized. *It could be anyone.*

He got into bed but slept fitfully, knowing that, a few feet below him, a cold heart rested.

Rory and Izzy stood upon the edge of a great cliff.

A vast sea was beneath them, with water so black and still it seemed like a mirror.

Rory looked out over the water. A dark cloud — purple and black and pulsing with lightning — slowly drifted toward them.

Inside the cloud, a shape writhed to and fro, a living mass of black liquid churning and turning in on itself.

It began to grow arms and hands and legs. A head listed back and forth, as if trying to gain control of its newborn body. Where its mouth should have been was a void. Red flames danced within it.

I thirst, *a woman's voice called.* I hunger.

Rory awoke at dawn, his breath coming fast.

He was sweating.

He threw off his thin blanket. Most nights it was cold in the small room, but tonight it was hot. He got up and walked over to the basin to wash his face. He shook his head. The water was black. He'd been too tired to empty it earlier.

His thoughts were muddled. He knew he'd just had a terrifying dream, but it was slipping away second by second. He pulled off his shirt, damp with sweat, and tossed it on the bed. He had changed his clothes as often as he could at Foxglove Manor but had only thoroughly washed them once, with water he'd heated in the kitchen. Malvonius had scolded him, of course, and told him to not use too much. How was he supposed to wear clean clothes if he couldn't wash them properly? Just another reason he despised the creepy man.

Rory licked his lips. He needed water. His throat was parched and dry. And that's when he remembered:

A shapeless shadow, trying to gain a human form.

I thirst. I hunger.

It was the strangest dream he'd ever had.

He crept along the upstairs hall quietly. *If I find you in a part of the house where you are not expected again, I'm afraid our little arrangement will come to an end.*

Rory made his way down the stairs. All he wanted was something to drink. Why should he have to sneak just for that?

He poked his head around the door to the kitchen.

Empty.

He walked in and stood over the sink, then turned on the tap slowly, making sure it didn't creak. Cool water poured out and spilled into the basin. Rory splashed his face, then took a tin cup from the counter and filled it to the brim. It felt cool and sweet going down his throat, and he relished the moment, drinking greedily. Briefly, he thought to listen at the red door but once again resisted. *What is in there?* he wondered.

"Wandering about again, are we?"

Rory froze.

He turned around slowly, still holding the cup.

Malvonius stood with one hand behind his back.

"I was thirsty," Rory said quietly.

"I see," Malvonius replied. "And why are you not dressed? Are you a savage of some sort?"

Only then did Rory realize he was bare chested but for the black stone he wore around his neck. He hadn't put his damp shirt back on before creeping downstairs. "I . . ."

"It is of no consequence," Malvonius said, cutting him off. "There are more important matters to discuss."

He withdrew his hand from behind his back. "What, pray tell, do you know of this?"

Rory dropped his cup.

It was the black box.

Malvonius pinched Rory's ear and marched him down to Lord Foxglove's dark cellar.

"Owww!" Rory cried, trying to squirm away.

But Malvonius didn't let go. Rory thought for a moment of making a run for it, but there was no way that would work. The butler's arms and legs were way too long, and Rory'd be caught in an instant, like a fly trapped by a spider.

He stumbled on the bottom step, but Malvonius yanked him along until they were standing outside of Foxglove's study. In the midst of his distress, with his heart beating furiously, the carvings in the wood stood out to him—a woman's face, with leaves and vines for hair. He'd seen them before, but not this close. He tried to examine them, but Malvonius opened the doors without knocking and pushed Rory forward, sending him to his knees. The blood rushed to his face.

"Stand up!" Malvonius shouted.

Rory got up unsteadily, his kneecaps thrumming with pain. His ear stung where Malvonius had snagged him.

Lord Foxglove rose from his desk and walked forward. "What do we have here?" he said in a cold voice.

"I found this in his room," Malvonius said, offering the box.

Rory shuddered.

Lord Foxglove took the lacquered box. He caressed it with a long finger. "Curious," he said. "I'd almost forgotten."

Sweat trickled down Rory's back.

"Yes," Foxglove continued, still focused on the box. "Almost forgotten."

The lord of the manor finally turned his attention to Rory. "Did you know, Rory, that you are not the first valet to work in this most glorious house?"

Rory didn't answer. He sensed Malvonius behind him. The butler had pushed him. *Hard.* Rory promised himself he'd repay the favor someday.

"Yes," Lord Foxglove said. "Your predecessor was a boy named Timothy. Such a lovely child." His eyes roamed over Rory with a look of disdain. "He wouldn't be caught in such a state. Look at you. Half-dressed."

Rory was trembling now.

Foxglove turned away and began to pace. "Poor Timothy," he continued. "Light of foot, with hair as pale as an angel's. Alas, he went astray." He paused and turned to Rory again, and his face was monstrous. "Wandering about the house on his own without my permission!"

Rory cowered, almost bumping into the butler.

Lord Foxglove drew himself up, and his shadow on the wall grew with him. "And now, I'm afraid Timothy isn't with us anymore," he said casually. "Is he, Malvonius?"

"No, my lord," Malvonius said obsequiously. "I'm afraid not."

"But I do have something to remind me of him," Foxglove said, and then he opened the box. "His heart, Rory. I have his heart."

Rory turned and ran for the door.

Malvonius reached out quickly, pinning Rory's arms behind him.

"No!" Rory shouted, struggling. "Let me go!"

Lord Foxglove stepped closer. "Hmm," he said, still caressing the box. "What shall we do with him, I wonder."

"Let me go!" Rory cried out again.

Foxglove bent down so his face was mere inches from Rory's. "Do you remember the contract you signed?" he said softly. "There were some words along the bottom. 'Upon penalty of death,' it read. It stated that you were not to wander in the back garden at any cost, did it not?"

Rory didn't remember any such thing. He continued to

fight, squirming and twisting, but Malvonius held him tight. "You never said that!" he shot back.

"Regardless," Lord Foxglove said, rising back up, "you have broken our agreement. The penalty is death."

"No!" Rory shouted, and kicked back with his right heel, directly into Malvonius's shin.

The butler grunted and, for a second, loosened his grip, which gave Rory just enough time to make a run for it. He bolted away and dashed for the door.

"Seize him!" Lord Foxglove shouted.

Rory burst through the double doors and sprinted toward the steps. Up and up he went, pushing himself as fast as he could, but his knees throbbed from being thrown to the cold marble floor. His head spun from the dizzying spiral staircase. Malvonius's heavy footsteps pounded behind him.

Boom. Boom. Boom.

Rory reached the top, but a wiry hand with sharp fingernails gripped his ankle and pulled him back.

He fell, banging his chin on a step. Pain shot through him. Malvonius's nails dug into the bare skin of Rory's ankle.

"No!" Rory cried, and kicked with all of his might, sending Malvonius tumbling back down the stairs.

Rory scrambled to his feet and raced down the hallway, making a quick turn and heading for the front door.

A few more steps, he told himself. *Just a few more steps.*

Blood dribbled down his chin. His knees felt like they'd been hit by hammers.

He stumbled down the reception hall until he got to the end, then, without looking back, flung open the door and rushed into the street.

CHAPTER FOURTEEN

A Shoeless, Shirtless Boy

Rory rushed out into the daylight.

The salty taste of blood was on his lips. He was disoriented and stopped for a minute to rest, taking deep gulps of air. *Breathe,* he told himself. *Breathe.*

The main avenue of Gloom, the Strasse, was full of townspeople going about their morning tasks, but Rory didn't see any of them. He was in a fog.

Many people saw the shoeless, shirtless boy running down the street but were too afraid to help. They only looked on curiously and called out, "Are you all right, lad?" or, "That's Hilda's boy."

Rory didn't answer them.

I was right! It was a heart. A boy named Timothy. Foxglove and Malvonius killed him!

He made it to his house, his breath coming in gasps. He turned the knob.

Locked.

He banged on the door. "Mum!" he shouted. "Open the door!"

Only in the midst of calling out again did Rory realize where she probably was. *She must have a work day. At the leather tannery.*

He turned around.

He had to find Izzy.

Black Maddie's. She'd be there now, reading her carved deck for customers.

Rory turned around and headed back up the Strasse.

He rushed into Black Maddie's. The air was thick with smoke and the sour smell of spilled beer, even though noon had yet to arrive. The patrons turned from their drinks and conversation to stare at him. Rory didn't care. He shoved his way through the noisy crowd and toward the back.

Relief flooded through him as he saw his friend's familiar silhouette behind the red curtain. He swept it aside.

Izzy looked up, startled. "Great seas!" she exclaimed.

Izzy dabbed at the blood on Rory's chin with a rag she got from the barkeep. A too-large sweater hung on his small frame, courtesy of one of the patrons. His feet were still bare. Rory sat and grasped his cinnamon-root elixir, the cup warming his hands.

"They tried to do *what?*" Izzy asked in disbelief.

She'd taken her chair from behind the table and now sat alongside Rory.

"They said the penalty was death!" Rory spit out. "They're crazy!"

Izzy set the rag on the table. Her face was troubled. "A human heart?" she asked for the second time.

"Some poor kid named Timothy," Rory said. "For all we know, there could be more . . . hearts back there. We have to stop them! They could be murdering kids!"

"They *are* crazy," Izzy agreed. "They tried to hurt you. Are you sure you're okay?"

Rory didn't answer. He was shaking.

"We have to find out what's going on there," Izzy said.

Rory let out a long, unsteady breath. He did want answers to the mystery of the red door and Arcanus Creatura, but he also knew that digging any further could be extremely dangerous.

Silence passed between them, broken by the sound of someone singing on the stage. Rory fingered the stone around his neck. For a moment, the voice put him at ease, and he remembered something else he wanted to tell Izzy. "I saw some paintings at the manor," he started. "They were all done by the same artist. Someone named Lysander Swoop, in Captain's Quay."

"Okay," Izzy said, eager for more.

"Well, if this Swoop guy painted Foxglove, he might be able to tell us something about him. Where he comes from and stuff like that."

Izzy rubbed her chin—doubtfully, it seemed to Rory.

"Izzy!" he exclaimed. "I know something strange is happening. They have a red door that's always locked! Bones were on their dinner plates! *And* I found a human heart! By the sea gods!"

Izzy looked at Rory for a long moment.

"What?" he said.

"We'll do it," she finally said, lowering her voice. "I'll

go with you to find this . . . artist, but we have to be careful. We could end up in some kind of trouble. You know — *big* trouble."

She was right, Rory was certain. But he needed to know what was really happening at Foxglove Manor, especially if someone was killed there. "Good," he said. "My mum's friend Vincent said some strange things about that place, and Ox Bells said when he was in the circus, the ringmaster never came to this town because they were afraid of something there. What if it's all connected, and —"

"You in there?" a man's deep voice boomed through the curtain.

Rory bolted from his chair. "It's Malvonius," he whispered. "He found me!"

Izzy put her fingers to her lips and silently rose from her seat. She opened the case where she kept her carved deck and lifted the cards, then pulled out a knife with a whalebone handle. Rory looked at the gleaming blade gripped in her fist. Of course she had a weapon. He'd hate to be the person on the other end of it.

He looked at her and nodded. He knew what to do. They didn't even have to speak. He whisked the curtain aside and Izzy leapt forward, ready to strike.

"Bloody seas!" a small, rumpled man cried out, cowering. "Only want me fortune read, not to get gutted like a fish!"

Izzy sighed and lowered her arm. She looked to Rory and shook her head, relieved.

"Well," the customer said warily. "Ya reading fortunes tonight or not?"

Rory turned to Izzy. "Tomorrow," he said to her, slipping around the small man, toward the noisy room beyond. "Captain's Quay."

Izzy set the knife on her table. "Tomorrow," she replied, and invited the fortune seeker in.

CHAPTER FIFTEEN

Captain's Quay

Picking the lock was easy, now that his nerves were a bit calmer. He promised himself he'd find a better way to keep their house secure in the future. Now he sat on the couch in the front room, the only light provided by an oil lantern on the table. The soft glow pooled around him, as if creating a circle of safety. Every few minutes, he got up and peered out the window.

Do Foxglove and Malvonius know where I live? Who can stop them if they come after me? Maybe Ox Bells, but Ox Bells wasn't there. Rory was alone, waiting for his mum to return from her night shift at Black Maddie's.

He could have stayed with Izzy and waited there for her. She went to Black Maddie's to sing for the patrons right after her shift at the tannery. But Rory didn't think the inn would be a good place to tell her what he'd been through. They needed to talk alone.

A rustling outside made Rory stand up quickly.

The door opened with a creak. He tensed.

"Rory?" his mum called.

They sat together in the kitchen. The room was too small to hold his mum's rage.

"We'll show them," she said. "Lay a hand on my son! Ox Bells knows people, Rory. Oafs as big as he is. But he's loyal. And Cora too. Don't be fooled by her fancy clothes!" She rapped her knuckles on the table.

Rory had never seen his mum this angry before. Her cheeks were as red as her hair. Rory hadn't told her everything though, only that he'd been beaten for disobeying orders. He had to explain the cut lip, after all. It would have been too hard for her to believe the rest of it. Rory barely believed it himself—mysterious words behind a red door that seemed to be alive, the face of an animal on the butler, and a boy's heart found in the back garden.

No, Rory thought. *Just me and Izzy know what really happened.* It had to be just the two of them.

"What about the shirrifs?" his mum suggested. "We could send them over there and give Lord whatever-his-name-is a stern talking-to at the least."

Rory didn't want to get the shirrifs involved either. They were a group of men and women in Gloom who were supposed to make sure people upheld the law. More times than not, Rory saw them milling about in Black Maddie's, drinking pints of ale.

"No, Mum," he said, thinking quickly. "Lord Foxglove has money. And we don't. He'd probably just pay off the shirrifs anyway."

His mum nodded along, seeming to buy his reasoning.

She scowled. "Vincent was right. There *is* something strange going on in that house."

Rory was certain of that, but he couldn't let on that he knew more. It would only make matters worse and create more questions. Knowing his mum, she'd probably storm over to the manor and demand to see Foxglove herself. Rory didn't want that to happen. He couldn't even imagine what Foxglove and Malvonius would do if she approached them in anger.

"Well," his mum said, "at least we got a little money out of it, yeah?"

"Right," he said.

"And we're keeping every copper," she finished.

Rory lay on his bed. He breathed in deeply and then exhaled. He was home. It didn't have the luxuries of Foxglove Manor, but there was no place he'd rather be. Not that he'd ever experienced those luxuries anyway—they'd barely even let him bathe properly. Foxglove and Malvonius were terrible, terrible people. Would they really have tried to kill him?

Rory tried to picture Timothy, the poor boy who'd broken Foxglove's rules, but he couldn't. *That would just make it worse*, he thought. Timothy's face would plague his dreams, and he didn't need that. But still, he felt bad for the dead boy. Did his parents know what became of him? Were they hoping he would return someday?

Rory fell asleep with all of these thoughts fighting for space in his head.

The human shape grew larger with each passing moment. Tangled strands of hair floated away from its head, as if stirring in a breeze. Black birds swirled around the form, creating a whirlwind. The

figure lifted its shadowy arms. "I thirst!" it cried out as if in pain. "I hunger!"

Rory woke with a scream on his lips. At first he thought he was at Foxglove Manor, but the familiarity of his room brought him back to reality. He was home.

He breathed easier, but the dream lingered in his mind. It was like the other one he'd had, where he and Izzy were standing on a great cliff. He had forgotten to tell her about it in the midst of all the other madness.

Rory's mum peeked her head around the doorframe. "Time to wake up, sleepy bones. Food is getting cold."

He shook the dark thoughts away and got dressed.

Breakfast was fried fish and crunchy bread. Rory savored the taste. His mum watched him eat, and Rory could tell she was glad to have him back home. She even fried up another piece of fish.

When he'd finished, he rose from the table. "Thanks, Mum."

Hilda smiled and pulled him close. Rory inhaled the comforting fragrance of patchouli. He'd missed it. She held on to him for a long moment.

"Me and Izzy have something we need to do," he said, breaking the embrace.

His mum frowned. "Don't go getting in trouble," she warned. "Just leave that nasty business at the manor behind. Do you understand?"

"Of course, Mum."

She looked at him skeptically.

"Mum," Rory said flatly. "Don't worry."

She tilted her head in doubt, but a sympathetic smile betrayed her thoughts. "Just a minute." She pulled the picture frame from the wall, reached in the cubbyhole, and withdrew the jar. "You earned this money," she said, counting out some coins. "It's good to have a little in your pocket."

Rory held out his open palm and took it. She was right. He did earn that money, and he had every right to it.

"Thanks, Mum," he said, and kissed her on the cheek.

Rory and Izzy made their way down the Strasse. The air was cool and crisp, but the sky was as gray and leaden as every other day.

"Do you think we'll find him?" Izzy ventured. "This . . . Lysander Swoop?"

"We have to try," Rory answered. "He's the only one we know of who might be able to tell us something about Foxglove."

They walked in silence for a while. Vendors and shoppers crowded the streets, as well as a few stray dogs and cats, looking for food. The familiar smell of fresh fish rose on the air.

"I had a dream," Rory suddenly said, remembering what he wanted to tell her. "Twice now. Once at the manor and last night at home."

"What . . . kind of dream?"

"The first time it was the two of us, looking out over what I think was the Black Sea. A scary cloud was coming our way. It looked like something was inside of it . . . something trying to take shape. And then I heard a woman's voice say, 'I thirst. I hunger.'"

Izzy didn't speak for a moment. "I don't like the sound of that," she finally said. "You're sure it was a woman's voice?"

"I'm certain," Rory replied. "And last night, I had the dream again, but it was full of blackbirds. I heard the same voice crying out in pain."

And that's when Rory realized it.

"'She is coming,'" he recited. "'I can feel her upon the wind.' That's what I heard through the red door, Izzy! What if the voice in my dreams belongs to whoever this *she* is they were talking about?"

"Maybe," Izzy said doubtfully. "But Rory, why would you have a dream like that? Dreams of prophecy are usually seen by people with some kind of gift, like . . . magic."

A dog ran in front of them, and Rory jumped out of the way.

"Magic?" He almost laughed. "I don't think so, Izzy."

But the expression on Izzy's face said she thought otherwise.

It took nearly an hour to walk to Captain's Quay, and Rory was tired by the time they arrived. Izzy, on the other hand, seemed ready to walk for another hour.

Houses and storefront awnings displayed what had once been a rainbow of colors: red, green, yellow, and blue. Captain's Quay was near the dock that traders and merchants sailed into when they first arrived in Gloom, and Rory had heard that the citizens painted their houses in bright colors because they wanted to make a good impression. But over time, like most everything in Gloom, the color had leeched out of Captain's Quay, and it became like everywhere else in the town, dull and gray.

A boardwalk ran from one end of the neighborhood to the other. It was home to several businesses: mostly food sellers, fortune-tellers, and gambling dens. Rory saw a few boats out in the distance, on the Black Sea.

"We don't even have an address," Izzy said. "Where do we start?"

Rory stopped in the middle of the street and peered around. "Well," he said, "we know he's a painter, right? Where would an artist live?"

"Dunno," Izzy answered. "Some fancy house?"

Rory sighed. "Let's just walk a bit and see what we can find."

They made their way to the boardwalk, a wooden promenade where people strolled along glumly. Pigeon droppings littered the planks. They passed a woman selling fresh clams from a wooden stall.

"Mmm." Izzy swooned. "Let's get some. I'm hungry."

Rory thought he didn't have any money for a moment, but soon remembered. He fished in his pocket and came up with a few coins. The woman behind the counter, grim faced and thin with a tattoo of a squid on her forearm, shucked a few clams with lightning speed and handed them to Rory on a piece of flat stone. He slurped his down greedily, savoring the pungent ocean taste.

"Fresh," Izzy said, swallowing hers.

Rory wiped his fingers on his pants. He looked out toward the water. A lone figure stood on the stretch of beach that ran parallel to the boardwalk, a wooden easel propped up in front of him. Rory nudged his friend. "Look."

Izzy peered into the distance. "He's painting," she said. "Could it be?"

"C'mon," Rory replied.

They stepped off the boardwalk and onto muddy sand. Rocks and glass bottles littered the area. They approached the man warily. He looked to be intently focused on his work. A small canvas set upon a wooden easel revealed a half-painted seascape. He was a rotund man with bushy white eyebrows, the same color as his long hair, which blew slightly in the cool sea breeze.

"Excuse me, sir," Rory said softly.

The man looked up. He hadn't even seen them approach and now examined the two of them closely. Clear blue eyes looked out from a round face. A neatly trimmed white beard came to a point on his chin.

"Yes?" he asked.

Rory froze. What should he say? He had to tread carefully. He had no idea what this man's relationship to Foxglove could be. "Is your name Swoop?" he asked. "Lysander Swoop?"

The man narrowed his eyes at Rory and then glanced at Izzy. "Who are you?"

"I'm Rory, and this is Izzy —"

"We wanna know about a man named Foxglove," Izzy blurted out.

Rory winced.

"Who sent you?" the man demanded.

He's frightened, Rory thought. *He does know something.*

"I did what I was asked," the man said. "He . . . he said I was safe. Who are you?"

"No one sent us," Rory replied. "We just want to know more about him. Foxglove."

The painter quickly began to gather up his paints and brushes. "I do not know who you are," he said, kneeling, "but I have nothing to say about . . . about that. I know nothing. Do you understand?"

He carefully placed his small watercolor in a panel in the folding easel kit and then clicked it shut. "Now I must be going." He stood up. "Good day."

"Wait," Rory said. "Please."

The man paused. All was silent for a moment but for a lone seagull squawking above them.

"What can you tell us," Izzy said slowly, "about . . . Arcanus Creatura?"

It was as if the artist had been struck by lightning. A snaky vein throbbed on his forehead. Rory even thought he saw the man's hands tremble.

"You know?" the artist asked in a whisper, his eyes now wide. "About them? Who they are?"

Rory looked to Izzy and then back to the painter. "Kind of," he answered.

The man let out a desperate breath. "Follow me."

CHAPTER SIXTEEN

Upon Entering the House of Lysander Swoop

The painter, who was surely Lysander Swoop, led Rory and Izzy along the water's edge. He wasn't a tall man, but his strides were long and they had a hard time keeping pace with him, wading through high seagrass and stepping around mounds of sand and discarded glass bottles.

Izzy nudged Rory as they followed behind. "Did you hear him?" she whispered. "He knows something."

Rory nodded. "And he seemed terrified."

The man led them up from the water's edge and onto the boardwalk. There were only a few people there, solitary figures caught up in their own doldrums. A boy sold fish from a barrel of salt water. A woman spun cloth on a loom. Swoop stopped and turned around. He looked toward the other end of the promenade. "Around this corner," he said. "Hurry!"

Rory and Izzy shared an alarmed glance. *Were they being followed?*

The man led them along quickly, past an inn called Bertha's, where children stood out front begging for coin, their clothes in tatters. Rory's heart panged. There were hundreds like them in Gloom. One day, he thought, he'd like to help them, but he didn't know how.

They passed a sail-maker's shop, its green canvas awning above them flapping in the wind. Finally, they came to a street where rows of modest homes lined both sides. Most of them were rundown and shabby, but the one that Swoop led them to looked clean from the outside. Dead flowers littered the wooden planter. Rory felt bad looking at their faded petals. The artist took a chain from around his neck and unlocked the door. He looked left, then right, and then invited them in.

Rory was immediately assailed by the sharp odor of turpentine. Paintings covered every inch of wall space. A few sculptures rested on tables and in between books on shelves.

The man opened his easel kit and placed his unfinished canvas on its ledge. "Please," he said, "sit."

Rory and Izzy sat on a couch covered in a fabric of painted roses.

"Something to drink?" the artist offered. "Tea?"

"Sure," Rory replied. It didn't really seem like an occasion to drink tea, but the idea sounded nice. Perhaps it would help calm Swoop's nerves — and his own, Rory realized.

"Thanks," Izzy said.

The man disappeared around a corner. A few seconds passed before Izzy whispered, "Look at this place."

Rory scanned the room. Several of the paintings resembled the ones in Foxglove's main hall — portraits of men and women in various poses. There were others too: animals, seascapes, flowers in vases. In addition to the furniture and art, colorful tapestries were spread out on the floor. Rory spied patterns of flowers, bees at a hive, a woman holding two lanterns, and many more strange images. A table near the couch held spirits in green bottles.

Swoop returned bearing a tray balanced with tea and cups, and placed it on a low table between the couch and two chairs. He poured for each of them and then walked to the window. He peered out, looking both ways, and then drew the curtains shut. "How did you find me?" he asked, returning to sit in one of the chairs.

Rory looked to Izzy and then back to their host. "I was

working at Foxglove Manor as a valet. I needed the money, see. It's just me and my mum, so I took the job."

Swoop almost spilled his drink. "You went there . . . willingly?"

"Yeah," Rory answered. "I didn't know anything about Foxglove or the house, but when I got there, weird stuff started happening."

"*Really* weird stuff," Izzy added.

Swoop nodded. "Tell me more."

Rory took a sip of tea. He looked to Izzy, who nodded in encouragement.

And then, he started talking.

It poured out of him in a rush, and with every revelation, he felt more and more relief. He told Swoop about the terrible shadow dream — the shapeless form that cried out, *I thirst. I hunger.* He recalled with dread the birdlike face he saw on Malvonius and the bones in the great room. He recited the words he'd heard behind the red door and spoke of how he'd found Swoop's signature on the paintings. Finally, after pausing to sip his now-cold tea, he mentioned the human heart in the back garden and his escape.

As Rory talked, Izzy cradled her cup and listened with wide eyes, as if she, too, were hearing his tale for the first time.

Through it all, the artist sat very still. Finally, he reached for his teacup and took a small drink, then set it back down. "My name *is* Lysander Swoop," he said. "I did indeed paint those portraits of Antius Foxglove and the others many years ago. I had to. I had no choice."

"Antius," Rory whispered.

"Okay," Izzy replied. "But what's so frightening about that? That's what you do for a living, right? Paint people's pictures?"

"I wish it were that simple, my child, but it is not."

Rory saw Izzy bristle at being called "child." It was only a small twitch along her jawline, but he knew her well enough to catch it.

"You see," Swoop went on, "at one time, I was the most prolific painter in all of Europica. People came from far and wide to buy my works." He lifted his head a little higher, thrusting out his bearded chin. "I was known as the royal portraitist for the Chevalier of Mercia."

Rory had heard of the continent of Mercia but didn't know much about it. It was a land that was supposedly filled with marvels: lights that came on with the flick of a switch, carriages that ran on some sort of liquid, and many more hard-to-believe inventions.

Swoop's proud pose slowly crumpled. "But then, I was commissioned by Foxglove to paint his portrait, as well as those of his . . . compatriots. Only the greatest painter in the world should be granted the privilege to paint his likeness, he demanded, and that is what I did."

Izzy frowned. "Still don't get it."

Swoop met her eyes and then lowered his voice. "For many years, I had heard rumors about Foxglove and his companions. That they held secret ceremonies. That they dabbled in some sort of dark arts"—he paused—"and that if you ever crossed them, you would pay with your life."

Rory gulped. *Upon Penalty of Death.*

Swoop sat back and swept a hand through his white hair. "That is why I painted their portraits. I didn't want anything to do with them, but Foxglove said he would take something from me if I did not agree."

"Take what?" Izzy and Rory asked at the same time.

Swoop let out an exhausted breath. "My shadow."

"Your . . . shadow?" Rory repeated.

"Yes," the painter replied.

"How could somebody take a shadow?" Izzy scoffed. "And if they could, what would they even do with it?"

"I had the same questions," Swoop replied, "so I began to do some research."

He sighed and stroked his beard. "Years ago, before I became a painter for hire, I traveled far and wide. I met a woman on the Isle of Bird who was versed in the ways of the old world. She told me stories of shadow reavers and daemons, spirits and summoners. There are old stories like this, in Gloom and elsewhere, child. Stories of mages and magic." He paused and swallowed nervously. "One night . . . one night, she showed me my own soul."

"What does this have to do with Foxglove saying he would take your shadow?" Rory asked.

Izzy nodded in agreement, as if she had the same question.

Lysander Swoop stood up. "The woman also told me something else. She said that from the moment we are born, our shadow is with us. It contains the stuff of life, our essence. Our shadows are guardians."

Rory sat motionless. He really didn't see what shadows had to do with anything. "Like . . . a soul?" he ventured.

Swoop walked to the bookshelf and picked up a small clay bird. "It is . . . different than the soul," he said, studying the sculpture as if it held a clue. "More . . . *tangible.* More . . . *solid.*"

Rory shook his head. *How could a shadow be stolen?*

"My carved deck says shadows are good fortune," Izzy said. "Like protectors of a sort."

"Exactly," Swoop replied, setting the bird back down, "and without a protector, we are all alone in this world. Unguarded."

Rory turned to Izzy, then back to Swoop. "Foxglove—how would he do it? Steal your shadow?"

The artist's face paled. "As I said, he and his minions deal in the dark mysteries. I believe they are sorcerers of some kind, bending people to their will. That is why I painted his portrait, as well as those of his associates. I never thought of them again until you . . . accosted me while I worked."

Izzy rolled her eyes.

Swoop sat back down. He seemed full of nervous energy, Rory noticed. *Fidgety.*

"What happens if a shadow is stolen?" Rory asked. "What then?"

"I would imagine you'd become a wraith," answered Swoop. "A shade of your former self."

"Like a ghost," Izzy said quietly.

They sat in silence.

"What about the words I heard through the closed red door?" Rory pressed him. "They said something about a great harvest, and that *she* was coming . . . that they could feel her upon the wind. Do you know what any of that means?"

Rory thought Swoop flinched at the question, but his only answer was a shake of his head.

He's hiding something, Rory thought. His hand went to his necklace and the black stone he wore.

"I have one piece of advice for you children," Swoop said, which Rory took as a sign that their meeting was almost over.

"What?" Izzy asked.

Lysander Swoop leaned forward in his chair and his eyes grew wide. "Stop asking questions. And never . . . *ever* . . . go anywhere near Foxglove Manor again."

CHAPTER SEVENTEEN

A Procession of the Most-Curious Sort

Rory and Izzy walked home quietly along the beach that ran parallel to the boardwalk. The sky above threatened rain. Rory reflected on all he had just learned. Foxglove and Malvonius were some sort of dark magicians. All the talk of shadows and magic only created more questions—one in particular, he wanted an answer to immediately.

He stopped walking and turned to Izzy. "I've seen you do things, Izzy. I know you have some kind of . . . gift." He paused. "Are you a witch, like you said that one time? If you are, now's the time to tell me."

Izzy curled a strand of hair around her finger, something she always did when being secretive.

"C'mon, Izzy," Rory urged her.

"My mum told me never to talk about it," she said in a rush.

"About what?"

She bit her lip.

"Izzy," Rory pressed her.

It seemed to Rory that she was struggling with how to answer. "It's true," she finally said, lowering her voice. "My mum's a witch, and her mum before her. Mostly just healing and herb lore, but once . . . she told me how to cast a spell."

"I knew it!" Rory exclaimed.

"Shh!" Izzy hissed. "Not so loud."

"You're special, Izzy."

"Don't feel special," she moaned. "Mum says I have something called 'the sight,' but I've never really tried to use it."

Rory's eyes grew larger. "Well, we have to figure it out. Maybe you can use it to stop Foxglove and whatever it is they're doing. It's bad, I know that much."

They started to walk again, the soft sand beneath their feet slowing their pace. The air was cooler now, and Rory wished he'd brought a coat.

"Dark magicians," Izzy said quietly. "Shadows. What could Foxglove be up to?"

"The answer's in the words I heard," Rory said. "Through the red door."

"*More*," Izzy said. "What do they need more of?"

The answer struck Rory like a bell that had just rung. "Shadows," he said.

They both stopped walking again and faced each other.

Izzy nodded as she began to speak, as if figuring it out right at that moment. "If shadows have some kind of . . . life essence, then maybe Foxglove wants shadows to . . . do what?"

"'I thirst,'" Rory said. "'I hunger.'"

"Hunger for shadows?" Izzy ventured.

Rory exhaled a shaky breath. "Shadows for whoever *she* is."

A slight rain began to fall, but not hard enough for them to seek shelter. Dark clouds thundered over the water.

"What was that?" Izzy whispered.

Rory snapped his head left, then right. "What?"

"Listen," Izzy said quietly.

A slight tinkling of bells rose in the air and floated around them, followed by the *rat-a-tat-tat* of a drum echoing down the beach.

Rory squinted, trying to get a better look. Shadowy figures were heading their way.

"C'mon!" he cried out, grabbing Izzy's arm and pulling her away, underneath the boardwalk.

"What in the world is it?" she asked.

"I just hope it's not them," Rory said, looking out from under the walkway. "You know, Arcan—"

"Don't even say their name," Izzy warned.

The mysterious shapes drew closer. Raucous laughter rang out.

Rory still held Izzy by the arm, ready to flee or fight, he didn't know which. But as they watched from the safety of their hiding place, a curious procession passed before them. At the head of it, a man with bare, tattooed arms spewed flames from his mouth. Behind him came even stranger sights: accordionists, cymbal crashers, bell ringers, jugglers, men on stilts, magnificent horses, women in feathered masks, and, most delightful of all, a dozen child acrobats leaping and jumping. Stray dogs had even fallen in behind the group, barking and wagging their tails in excitement and slipping in the sand.

"What is it?" Rory asked. "Who are they?"

"It's a troupe," Izzy replied, wonder in her voice. "A carnival's coming to Gloom."

CHAPTER EIGHTEEN

Oxtail and Cabbage Soup

Rory sat with his mum in their small kitchen. The smell of oxtail and cabbage soup filled the room. It wasn't one of Rory's favorite meals, but it was easy to prepare and the ingredients didn't cost a lot. They still needed to stretch their money as far as they could. Yesterday's revelations weighed heavily on his mind.

Rory's mum placed a hot bowl in front of him.

"Thanks, Mum," he said glumly.

She sat down at the table, facing him.

"What is it?" she asked, perceptive as always.

Rory stirred his soup but didn't bring the spoon to his mouth.

"Mum, you've been in Gloom a long time, right?"

Hilda cocked her head. Her long hair was braided today, a style Rory thought made her look like a kid. She wasn't *that* old, she always told him. "Oh," she said, as if taken by surprise. "I've been in Gloom all my life, Rory. Only place I've ever known. You knew that, didn't you?"

Rory looked into his soup as if he could find an answer there. "Yeah. I guess so." He paused. "But what about Foxglove Manor? How long has it been here?"

Hilda flushed at the mention of the manor.

"What they did to you is a crime, Rory. I was reconsidering calling on the shirrifs."

Rory squirmed in his chair. Now that he knew how truly dangerous Foxglove was, he had to be extra careful. If not, more hearts might get buried, just like poor Timothy's.

"I don't want anyone else getting hurt," he said. "You said to put it behind me, right?"

Hilda nodded. "Suppose I did. But that still doesn't make it right." She raised her spoon to her mouth. "Lord Fancy Pants will get what's coming to him one of these days. I'm sure of it."

They ate their soup in silence for a few minutes. It felt good to be home, Rory thought, even with all of the madness surrounding him. "Me and Izzy saw something interesting," he offered.

"What's that?"

"A bunch of players, like a carnival. Have you heard anything about it?"

"A carnival? No, don't think so. I'll have to ask Ox Bells. He might know."

Rory was attempting to appear as if everything was normal. But it wasn't. A group of dark magicians was planning something evil.

A question came to him suddenly. "Mum, who's the oldest person in Gloom?"

Hilda looked up from her soup. "Well, you're quite inquisitive tonight, aren't you?"

Rory didn't answer.

His mum pushed her bowl away. "Too much pepper," she said fussily. She fiddled with one of her braids, then let out a breath. "Well," she started, and then paused. She tilted her head and narrowed her eyes. "Rory. What are you up to now? Something with Izzy, I suppose?"

"We were just wondering," Rory said, trying to sound like he didn't care one way or another. He sipped his soup.

Hilda put one elbow on the table and propped her chin in her palm, thinking. She drummed her fingers along her jaw. "Let me see. I suppose it would be Lyra Blanton. She's been here as long as I can remember."

"Blanton," Rory murmured.

"You've seen her. She's down at the market every day, selling those sad flowers."

An image appeared in Rory's mind—an old woman with silver hair pulled back in a single braid. He'd passed her by every time he went shopping. "Okay," he said. "Thanks, Mum."

Hilda went back to her soup, but not before casting another inquiring look at her son.

As for Rory, he had an idea.

And he had to tell Izzy.

CHAPTER NINETEEN

A Faded Tulip

Rory and Izzy bustled through the crowds at Market Square. The sky was dark, with ominous gray clouds rolling in. "What are we doing again?" Izzy asked.

"If Lyra Blanton is the oldest person in Gloom," Rory replied, "maybe she knows how long Foxglove Manor has been here."

"And what would that tell us?"

A horse-drawn cart full of barrels rattled by, and Rory stepped out of the way, narrowly avoiding a puddle of some foul substance.

"I'm not sure," he said. "But we need to learn everything

there is about Foxglove. The more we know, the better chance we have of finding out what they're planning."

Izzy nodded, tight-lipped and serious.

The table in front of Lyra Blanton's stall was a sad display. A few plants looked somewhat healthy, but the flowers in vases were on their last breath of life.

"Well, hello there, young ones," the old woman greeted them. "Can I interest you in a beautiful tulip?" She ran her fingers along a green vase with a single faded bloom.

"Um," Rory stuttered. "My mum told me you've been in Gloom a long time. Is that right?"

Lyra Blanton looked at him curiously. Her face was lined, but her eyes were clear and bright. A small ring with a turquoise stone stood out on her left hand. "You're Hilda's boy?"

"Uh, yes." Rory was taken aback. He looked nothing like his mum, so he wondered how she knew.

"I've seen your mum sing at Black Maddie's," Lyra explained.

"Oh," Rory replied.

"And a beautiful voice she has too. Lovely as a siren."

Rory had heard of sirens, but he didn't know if it was a good thing to be compared to one. He swallowed. Peddlers jostled behind him, calling out daily specials.

"And you're Pekka's little girl. Is that right?"

Izzy nodded, somewhat grudgingly.

"I have a question for you," Rory tried again. "Me and Izzy were wondering: Do you know how long Foxglove Manor's been here?"

Lyra Blanton's cheery demeanor faded. Her clear eyes grew wet.

Rory flushed, embarrassed. "I'm sorry. I didn't mean to . . ."

Lyra sat heavily on a stool behind her. She took a silk cloth from her pocket and dabbed her eyes. "Just a little lad, he was. My Timothy."

Rory froze.

Such a lovely child. Light of foot, with hair as pale as an angel's.

Izzy gasped, but Lyra Blanton was too caught up in her memory to notice.

"Timothy?" Rory asked. He had to tread carefully. He didn't want to cause the woman any more distress.

"Yes, my Timothy," she went on, a weak smile forming on her face. "Lovely, fine hair. Like a fairy, he was. Had an accident up there at the big house. Was stuck in the chimney when he tried to clean it." She laid a wrinkled hand on her heart. "Injured his poor chest." She dabbed at her eyes again. "They gave his body back," she whispered. "So small . . . so small."

Izzy gave the woman a moment to gather herself. "And there wasn't anything . . . fishy about it?" she asked.

Lyra Blanton released a huge sigh. "No. Not really. It was dangerous work in those days, being a chimney sweep."

"I'm sorry," Rory said, biting back his anger. Foxglove had lied to Lyra Blanton. He was an evil, evil man. *No, not man,* Rory thought. He didn't know what he was.

He still wanted more answers. "So, the manor. Do you know how long it's been in Gloom? And Lord Foxglove? What do you know about him?"

Rory waited. He hoped he wasn't making things worse, dragging up painful memories in this woman's mind. But much to his surprise, she smiled affectionately.

Izzy's eyebrows rose.

"Ah, a good man," the old woman said. "Gave me and my late husband enough money and plenty more to bury poor Timothy. Rich, he is. Bought the town long ago, so long ago now no one remembers."

Rory stared, stricken.

Izzy's mouth literally formed an *O* before she quickly closed it.

"Bought the town?" Rory asked cautiously.

"Oh yes," Lyra Blanton said. "Paid for the town's new land

deed. Have you never heard? This town wasn't always called Gloom."

Rory felt as if his legs were about to buckle.

"What . . . did it *used* to be called?" Izzy asked.

Lyra Blanton looked past them, as if she were seeing another place and time in her memory. "A nice town, it was. Sea Bell, it was called. If you go down to the dock, past the Squid and Anchor, you can see some of the old mariners' bells they used to ring to announce ships coming in."

Rory and Izzy stood silently.

Around them, merchants shouted, dogs barked, small children wailed. But they were oblivious.

Gloom. Sea Bell.

"So what else can I be helping you with?" Lyra Blanton's voice broke Rory's trance.

"Um. Nothing. Thanks. We appreciate it."

Izzy fished in her pocket and laid a few coins on the counter. "Is this enough? For the tulip?"

The gesture was so kind Rory thought his heart would break.

A smile grew on the old woman's lined face. "Of course, dear," she said, handing Izzy the vase with the faded flower.

Izzy laid a hand on Lyra Blanton's shoulder. "We're sorry,"

she said. "I'm sure Timothy was a fine boy. We won't forget about him. Will we, Rory?"

"No," Rory said, and his voice was distant in his ears. "We won't."

CHAPTER TWENTY

Saved by a Curse

"Sea Bell," Rory said. "Not Gloom. *Sea Bell.*"

His head was spinning from Lyra Blanton's revelations. "Foxglove named the town Gloom. Did he think that was funny?"

"That boy didn't get stuck in a chimney," Izzy shot back. "Foxglove killed him and buried his heart!"

"What if Timothy wasn't the only one?" Rory said. "What if there are others? What if another boy or girl shows up to work there and they end up dead too?"

"All just more reasons to stop him," Izzy said.

Their thoughts had been coming so fast and furious they

barely knew they had left the market behind and were walking along the docks.

"We need to go see the painter again," Izzy suggested. "Swoop."

"Why wouldn't he have told us Foxglove owns the town?" Rory asked.

"Maybe he's still hiding something," Izzy said, an edge to her voice. "The little weasel."

Rory recalled Swoop's fidgeting and evasive manner. He knew more than he'd let on. He had to. "Tomorrow," he said. "Tomorrow we go back to Swoop's and press him for more information."

"Right," Izzy said. She made a gesture with her fingers. "And if he doesn't tell us, I'll curse him."

Later that day, Rory found himself at Market Square once again, doing some shopping for his mum. The dark clouds he had seen earlier never did bring rain, only a heaviness that seemed to weigh all of Gloom down. It had been like that for the past several days, Rory realized. Storm clouds brewing on strong winds.

He froze.

She is coming. I can feel her upon the wind.

He shook the thought away.

He cut down Quill Street, a small side alley that made the trip home a bit shorter. The fresh fish and oysters he carried in his sack gave off a pungent scent.

"Whatcher got there, eh?"

Rory stopped dead in his tracks. He turned around.

Canaries. Three of them. All in their yellow slickers and black caps.

Rory stopped breathing.

"What's the little cubby got?" one of them said.

They had a peculiar way of talking, the Canaries, with odd slang words that only they could decipher.

Rory backed up a step. He couldn't remember the last time he'd gotten into a fight, but it certainly wasn't with more than one opponent. A vendor came out of his shop, took one look at what was happening, and rushed back inside.

One of the Canaries stepped forward. His eyes were as small as a bird's. "Empty yer pockets, lovey," he said in a sickeningly sweet voice. "Giver up."

"No!" Rory said. His heart was racing. He crouched, ready to flee or charge, he wasn't sure which.

The leader smiled. He had a gap in the center of his teeth as big as a sausage. "Oi! He's full o' pepper, eh?"

"Get him!" yelled another.

"Make him sing, innit? Just a nick!"

The click of switchblades sounded in Rory's ears.

He dropped his bag, but before he could do anything, he saw a small, shadowy figure creeping up behind the Canaries.

"Oi!" Izzy's voice called out. "My mum's a witch, and she'll curse you if you don't leave him alone!"

Now, there's one thing about the Canaries that everyone knew. For all their bluster and violence, they were deathly afraid of anything that didn't seem quite *normal*. They'd seen Izzy at Black Maddie's, reading fortunes, and steered clear of her, assuming she was a witch of some sort. A "conjurer," they'd called her, a "trickster wench."

The Canaries all turned quickly, prepared to face this new threat.

Izzy began to tie her red hair up in a knot, a sign that she was ready to fight. But she didn't fight. She began to whisper. She walked forward one small step at a time, hunched over to make her approach even more menacing, snapping her fingers as she advanced.

"Black as night, black as coal,
   a witch's brew to steal the soul.

Slackety clap, clipety clak.

Better run now

and don't look back!"

Izzy crossed her fingers on both hands and extended her arms, pointing directly at the Canaries' leader.

The gang bolted in all directions, leaving Rory in the middle of the road.

Izzy watched as they disappeared. "Good thing I came along, eh?" she said.

Rory breathed a sigh of relief and picked up his bag. "Stupid Canaries," he said quietly. He stared at her for a long moment. "Wait. Where did you come from?"

Izzy chuckled. "I was on my way to Black Maddie's and I saw them tracking you, so I hung back and kept an eye on them. I had a feeling they might try something."

"It was the sight," Rory said eagerly. "That thing you said you have. You knew what was going to happen!"

Izzy rolled her eyes. "That's not the way it works. It's different than that."

"Well, what is it, then?"

They were interrupted as a lamplighter made his way up the street carrying a pole at least five feet long. At one time, every lamppost in Gloom was lit this way, but eventually, more and more gas lamps took their place. Now only a few still stood, a relic of another era. *Sea Bell,* Rory thought. *A nice town,* Lyra Blanton had called it.

A small flame danced at the end of the lamplighter's pole. Rory and Izzy watched as the man raised it to the glass globe at the very top. The round glass ball flickered and then illuminated the street with a weak yellow glow. The light spilled along the cobblestones where Rory stood. He looked down. "Izzy," he said.

"Yeah?"

Rory waved his arm in the air.

"My shadow. Where is it?"

Izzy looked to her feet, where a diagonal shaft of light stretched out before her. She turned in a circle, then stretched out her arms and waved them over her head. Her face suddenly paled. She looked at Rory. "Where's *my* shadow?" she said, her voice almost panicked. "By the sea gods, Rory! Where's my shadow?"

CHAPTER TWENTY-ONE

Hidden

"Foxglove," Rory spat out. "He did it! Swoop was right! He's a shadow stealer!"

Izzy sat on the ground and put her head in her hands.

"What's going to happen?" she asked. "We're gonna become . . . ghosts."

Rory shivered at the memory of Swoop's words: *I would imagine you'd become a wraith. A shade of your former self.*

"No," Rory said. "We're going to get our shadows back. Me and you, Izzy."

He offered his hand and she pulled herself up.

A man walked by and shot them a curious look. Rory

watched him pass and saw that he didn't cast a shadow either. "We have to do something," he said. "The whole town . . . everyone's shadow could be gone!"

"Foxglove," Izzy repeated, and the name sounded like a curse. "We're going there *now* to get our shadows back!"

Rory released a trembling breath. "Wait a minute," he said. "Let's get ahold of ourselves. We don't even know how to do that."

Izzy paced back and forth. "I can't believe it," she muttered.

Rory couldn't either.

He looked to the cobblestones again, lit by the lamplight. He waved his hand back and forth between the light and the ground. Nothing. There was no mirror image.

"Swoop," Izzy hissed. "Maybe he knows how. He was hiding something, Rory. I could tell."

Rory knew she was right. Plus, the artist was the one who'd talked about shadow stealing in the first place.

The idea of trying to retrieve his own shadow was beyond comprehension. Rory didn't even know where to begin. His eyes suddenly stung.

Izzy grabbed him by the shoulders. "We can do it, Rory. Foxglove stole our shadows and our town. He's going to get what's coming to him!"

Rory swallowed back tears. He didn't want to cry in front

of Izzy. "We're the only ones who can stop him," he said, voice trembling.

She released her grip, and the look she gave him was fierce. "And that's exactly what we're going to do."

Rory tossed and turned in bed, his thoughts plagued by visions of shadows and dark magicians.

My shadow, he thought, not for the first time. *Gone? How?*

He had heard his mother come in from her night shift at the tannery, but he was too fearful to go downstairs to see if she still had a shadow. What could he tell her? That he and Izzy would find a way to get them back?

He finally fell asleep, and his dreams were sunless and cold.

Rory and Izzy stood on the boardwalk of Captain's Quay. The wind was strong, and Rory watched a small boat rock to and fro on the bay while the captain struggled with a tattered sail.

Much to Rory's dismay, upon awakening, he had seen that his mum's shadow was, indeed, gone. She hadn't seemed to notice, though, only went about her morning tasks as usual. *I have to tell her,* Rory had thought. *No. I can't. Who knows how she'd take it? It's up to me and Izzy. We have to find a way.* Izzy had faced the same terrible realization when she had seen that Pekka's had vanished too.

The darkening skies that had been plaguing Gloom were even worse today. A cold wind came with them, screaming down the Strasse like a spirit. "Probably Foxglove's doing as well," Izzy said.

Now that Rory knew he didn't have a shadow, he constantly looked for it: along the road beneath his feet, on the side of every building he passed. It was gone.

Rory watched as people walked by, none of them casting any kind of shadow either.

"No one knows it's missing until they look," Izzy said distantly.

Will they all become wraiths? Rory wondered. *Like ghosts,* Izzy had said. What about his mum, and Izzy's?

"And these skies don't help," Rory replied, peering up at the black clouds. "I know Gloom is dark, but this seems . . . "

"Unnatural?" Izzy suggested.

A heavy silence hung in the air. The wind whipped along the boardwalk, sending paper and debris flying.

"She is coming," Rory whispered.

"I can feel her upon the wind," Izzy finished.

There was no sign of Swoop on the beach.

"Looks like we have to try his house," Izzy said.

They took the same path as they had before, past the inn called Bertha's and the sail-maker's shop. Rory walked warily, every now and then stopping to look behind them. *What if Swoop was right? What if he was being watched by someone? Were they being followed before, when they first met Swoop?*

Rory couldn't think about that now. They just had to find him and ask more questions: How could they get their shadows back? Did Foxglove and Malvonius have any weaknesses? And then there was the matter of Foxglove actually *owning* Gloom.

Rory shook his head at the strangeness of it all.

"This is it." Izzy's voice brought him out of his reverie.

They were standing on the steps of Lysander Swoop's house. Rory looked at the dead flowers and, once again, felt a sense of foreboding, a deep pang in his stomach. "Here goes," he said, and knocked on the door—three short raps.

A breeze came down the street, snapping the clothes drying on a neighbor's line.

"Maybe he's not home," Izzy said.

Rory knocked again, louder this time.

They waited, but there was no response. "What do you think?" he asked.

They both looked out to the street. They didn't want to draw suspicion. A spark suddenly gleamed in Izzy's eyes, one Rory had seen before — when she was up to no good.

She turned around again and faced the door, as did Rory. She rattled the knob, then peered in through the window. "Nothing," she said. "Curtain's in the way."

A moment of silence hung in the air between them.

Izzy took a pin from her hair and held it up.

"Really?" Rory asked in disbelief.

"Any better ideas?"

"No," he said, against his better judgment.

Izzy glanced back toward the street. "Stand behind me," she told him in a low voice. "Look like you're just waiting for someone."

Rory did as she asked. He released a trembling breath. He knew it was wrong to break in, but they needed answers, and he didn't know where else to find them.

He heard Izzy fiddling around with the keyhole and then a distinct click. "Got it," she said.

They entered quickly and shut the door behind them.

Rory gasped.

Lysander Swoop lay face-down on the floor, his arms and legs at crooked angles.

"Tears of a fish!" Izzy whispered.

Rory stepped forward carefully. Maybe Swoop was sleeping. Or drunk. He was an artist after all.

Rory knelt and took a deep breath, then gazed up at Izzy, who nodded. He rolled the man over.

Two lifeless eyes stared up at him.

He scrambled back. "He's . . . he's dead!"

Izzy didn't speak, but knelt next to the body. She lowered her ear to the artist's chest. Rory saw her blink calmly, as if in concentration. After a moment, she lifted her head. "Yup, he's dead, all right."

Rory closed his eyes and swallowed hard.

"I don't see any marks on him," Izzy observed, as if she saw dead bodies every day.

Magic, is what Rory was thinking, but kept it to himself.

"Uh-oh," Izzy said.

"What?"

She lifted Swoop's limp arm. Weak sunlight filtered in through the curtains. She moved the arm back and forth, as if he were a puppet, looking at the floor as she did so. "There's no shadow."

Rory stood up. He felt faint. His head spun. "They killed him *and* took his shadow."

"Or," Izzy countered, "they took his shadow and *then* killed him."

"We have to get out of here," Rory said nervously, peering around. Fear was slowly rising in his chest. Sweat beaded on his brow.

"Wait," Izzy said, rising from the floor. "Let's look around first. There might be something here we can use. Something that can help us get our shadows back."

Rory looked at his friend like she had truly lost her mind. "Are you mad? He's dead, Izzy. Dead. We can't . . . be here!"

Izzy didn't respond, only walked over to the wall and examined some of the paintings.

Rory sighed in frustration. He didn't want to look at Swoop's lifeless body again, but he did.

The man was dead.

"Check the books," Izzy called without looking at him. "There might be something there."

"Can't believe it," he muttered. "This is crazy." But still, he did as his friend said.

The rows of books on the shelves were broken up by a few small decorative objects between them. Rory picked up the clay bird that Swoop had handled just a few days ago. He placed it back down and angled his head to read some of the spines: *Lysander Swoop, Royal Portraitist; Goldenrod, Tales from the Sea; Ancient Rome: Myth or Reality?* Most of the other books were about painting and sculpture.

"Hey, look," Izzy said. "This is weird."

Rory walked over and stood beside her. His fear and frustration had lessened somewhat, but still, there was a dead body just over his shoulder.

He shivered.

Izzy had peeled away a sizable piece of loose rose-colored wallpaper between two of Swoop's paintings.

"It was flaking away," she said. "Look."

Rory leaned in. The distinct image of an eye stared back at him.

"What could it be?" he asked.

"Only one way to find out."

Izzy and Rory peeled away more of the wallpaper. It curled and fell to the floor in great ribbons. Rory glimpsed smudges of red, yellow, and green underneath. There was definitely a painting there.

At last, Rory peeled away the final strip.

"By the sea gods," Izzy whispered.

Rory didn't speak, but another tremor ran through him.

Staring back at them was the image of a woman. It looked as if Swoop had painted her in some sort of fever dream. The mouth was open, revealing red tongues of flame. The eyes were only smudges of color—more like the *impression* of human eyes. Twisted green and brown vines made up her hair.

Rory's dream flickered in his vision—a human form and red flames. He swallowed.

"Look," Izzy said, leaning in closer.

Rory took a tentative step forward. Along the bottom of the painting, a snaky line of red paint revealed a name.

"Mara," Rory whispered. He immediately felt as if he shouldn't have said the name aloud. "I've seen her before," he said quietly.

"Where?"

"My dream. I'm sure this is who I dreamed about. And it was also carved on Foxglove's cellar doors." He swallowed again. His mouth was dry. "This is her, Izzy. *She.*"

Izzy peered around the room warily, as if more hidden portraits were waiting to be discovered. "Why did Swoop paint this?" she asked.

"Why did he cover it up?" Rory shot back.

Izzy, while seemingly not distressed by the man's dead body, paled at the question.

Rory glanced away from the painting and then back again. It was hard to look at for more than a few seconds at a time. It was as if there was something in it that was pulling the viewer in, beckoning. Calling. "C'mon," he said abruptly. "Let's get out of here."

Izzy turned away from the wall. "What about him?" she

said, cocking her head in the direction of Lysander Swoop's crumpled form.

"I don't know," Rory replied. "We can't tell anyone. They'll want to know what we were doing here." He set his jaw. "*And we broke in.*"

"Just have to leave him then," Izzy said matter-of-factly.

Rory was taken aback by his friend's callousness, but he didn't know what to say. He was numb. He reluctantly walked to the door without glancing back, and imagined the eyes of Mara staring at his retreating form. *Who was she?*

"Wait," Izzy said, turning around.

"What?" Rory snapped. "We have to get out of here, Izzy. Now!"

She didn't answer, but walked to a table full of paints and brushes.

Rory joined her. "What are you doing?"

"I have an idea," she said.

Rory breathed in deeply. *We're never going to get out of here. We'll be caught, and then what will Mum do?*

Izzy picked up a small knife and walked back toward the image painted on the wall. To Rory's surprise, she began to scrape away some of the paint, cupping her free hand to collect the colored specks.

"What are you—" Rory started.

"Shh," Izzy scolded.

She continued to scrape until a small mound of paint was in her hand. Then she stepped away from the wall and looked at her open palm. She breathed in through her nostrils and then exhaled. "Okay. Let's go."

"What were you doing?" Rory asked. "What are you going to do with that?"

Izzy grinned. "I'm going to see if I really have the sight."

CHAPTER TWENTY-TWO

A Flame in the Dark

Night had fallen by the time they arrived at Black Maddie's. That's where Izzy wanted to do whatever it was she had planned. To see if she really had the sight. *Could it work?* Rory wondered.

The strangeness of the past few days plagued his thoughts. Was the shape in his dream Mara? The possibility filled him with dread. It was a woman's voice, after all, that had called out the ominous words: *I thirst. I hunger.* Why had he dreamt it? He pushed the possibility that he, like Izzy, might have magic to the back of his mind.

As they walked in silence, Rory saw that Izzy kept her

hand cupped, as if she were carrying an egg. A dog barked on the other side of the street and Rory jumped. His nerves were rattled.

They'd seen a dead body.

They'd even touched it.

If anyone had seen them go inside Swoop's house, they'd be in big trouble.

Rory opened the door to the inn and they stepped inside. People turned their heads and then went back to their drinks and conversation. *They don't know their shadows are gone,* Rory thought. A dim, smoky inn was the last place you'd expect to notice one.

Inside Izzy's little chamber, at her instruction, Rory lit the candles placed on the table. Soft yellow light pooled around them as they sat opposite each other. The noise and music from the front of the inn drifted back into the room. Rory still couldn't get the image of Mara out of his mind.

With a relieved breath, Izzy turned her hand over the table, letting the specks of paint fall onto the surface. She then reached into the drawer, pulled out a blank page of parchment, and laid it alongside the little mound of colored flakes.

"Izzy?" Rory asked. "Are you going to tell me what you're doing?"

She swept a lock of hair behind her ear. "I've seen my mum do some things," she began. "People come to the house now and then looking for answers: names of people they want to take revenge on, stuff like that. I've watched her, and she always tells people to bring something that belongs to them, so she can kind of . . . I don't know. Read it?"

Rory nodded. "Makes sense," he offered. "I guess?"

"Here goes," she said, and spit in her hand.

Rory raised an eyebrow. "What—?"

"Shh."

With her free hand, Izzy swept the paint flecks onto her wet palm and then rubbed both palms together.

"Lovely," Rory said.

Izzy ignored him. She drew her hands apart, smudged with color. "See?" she said, holding them up.

Rory nodded, intrigued.

Izzy placed one of her palms down on the paper.

She closed her eyes and whispered:

"Daughters of air,
daughters of smoke,
goddess of time and goddess of hope,
sky and fern and wood and water,
show me the sight I need, Mother-Daughter."

Rory had never heard her sound so serious.

She opened her eyes and lifted her hand.

Rory looked at Izzy's multicolored handprint on the parchment. They stared at it for what seemed like a very long time.

"What's supposed to happen?" he asked.

Izzy laid her other hand back over her own handprint. "Mara," she said. "Show us who she is."

As she spoke the name, Rory's heart bounced around in his chest. Like before, he sensed that saying it aloud was breaking some kind of rule. Or asking for trouble. He couldn't explain it, but it felt . . . *wrong.*

Izzy lifted her hand again.

And the paper burst into flame.

"Look out!" Rory cried, and pushed back from the table. But as suddenly as the flame appeared, it whooshed out, leaving only a wispy trail of smoke. Izzy and Rory watched in terrified fascination. The smoke hovered unnaturally over the table and around the pile of burned paper. Then it began to swoop and curl, as if guided by an invisible hand.

"It's writing," Izzy said calmly. "The goddess heard my call."

Rory shook his head. "It can't be," he whispered.

The smoke curled and turned as fluidly as a quill on

paper. Lines of script hovered an inch above the table. "Can you read it?" he asked.

"Not yet," said Izzy without looking away.

Rory felt as if he were in a dream. His head was heavy on his neck. A last wispy trail of smoke rose and then vanished. Rory heard his heartbeat in his ears.

Izzy and Rory looked at each other. They both tentatively leaned toward the table until they were almost touching heads.

"Mara of the Shadows," Izzy read the smoky words. "Beware, daughter. She is the Destroyer. Queen of Sorrow."

Rory licked his lips. His tongue was dry in his throat again. He read on, his voice unsteady. "She comes with the night. Mara of the Shadows . . ."

He drew back.

He didn't want to say the next words aloud.

So Izzy read them for him: "She thirsts. She hungers."

The smoke spun into black ribbons and then vanished.

CHAPTER TWENTY-THREE

An Almost Normal Day

Rory and Izzy stared across the table at each other.

"Those are the words, Rory," Izzy declared. "The words you heard in your dream."

"I know," he said, strangely calm. "Why did I dream it? Why did I hear it?"

Izzy ran a finger along the table. All signs of the smoke were gone, leaving just the remnants of the burned paper. "I don't know. Maybe you do have magic."

"*You* have the sight," Rory pointed out, ignoring what she had just said. He didn't want to think about it. It was too much.

They sat in silence. Rory didn't know what to say. A goddess had just given them a message. His world was turning upside down. "I need something to drink," he finally said.

Izzy rose from the table and passed through the red curtain. Rory felt cold. He couldn't believe what he had just seen.

Izzy had the sight, and she'd discovered who it was he'd seen in his dreams—the person Lysander Swoop had painted on his wall. Mara of the Shadows.

What did she want with him? Why had he dreamed of her?

Izzy returned with a cinnamon-root elixir. She studied him a moment before offering it. "You okay?"

"Yeah," Rory said absently, although he felt nothing of the sort.

"Here," she said, handing him the drink.

He took it eagerly. "Thanks."

Izzy walked around him and sat back down at the table. Candlelight flickered on her face. "The goddess said to beware."

"Goddess," Rory echoed. He shook his head. "What is happening, Izzy? How did we—how did all of this happen?"

"I don't know," Izzy replied. "But we can't stop now. We

know that Foxglove killed that boy, Timothy, and we have to get our shadows back."

"Not just ours," Rory said, thinking of his mum. "Everyone's in Gloom."

"Sea Bell." Izzy corrected him.

Somehow, he found himself half smiling. "Right. Sea Bell."

"We've gotta get in there," Izzy declared. "Into the manor."

Rory studied his feet for a moment and then looked back up. "I know."

Rory barely slept, and when he did, his dreams were filled with the image of a face made from nightmares.

Mara of the Shadows.

I thirst. I hunger.

She is coming. I can feel her upon the wind.

Was she coming to Gloom? What did she want?

We will need more. Much more.

More shadows? Rory wondered. Lysander Swoop also troubled Rory's dreams, the painter's cold, dead eyes staring up at him.

He was dead.

Dead.

Surely killed by Foxglove and Arcanus Creatura.

Were they going to come for Rory too?

He rose from bed. The night had passed quickly. He and Izzy had to stop Foxglove. No matter what.

But can we do it? Even if Izzy did have some kind of special witch powers, how could she possibly stand up against them?

Rory recalled the words he'd heard behind the red door.

A great harvest is coming.

Was this shadow-stealing the harvest? It had to be. What else could it have meant?

Rory sighed and put on his clothes. If they were really going into Foxglove Manor, he'd have to protect himself. He retrieved a dagger from the drawer of his bedside table. He'd used it to whittle wood when he was younger, carving little animals and flowers. Ox Bells had shown him how. It wasn't much of a weapon, but he felt safer with it.

He slipped it into his boot.

Rory looked in the small piece of mirror glass nailed to the wall. His reflection peered back at him. He realized he hadn't really seen himself in a long time. His eyes were bleary, and he thought they didn't have the same sparkle to them as they'd had before — before he'd met Antius Foxglove and Malvonius Root, that is.

Downstairs, his mum, Ox Bells, and Miss Cora were in the sitting room drinking tea.

"There he is," Ox Bells called out. "Your mum says you've been in and out like a shadow these past few days. Whatcher been doing, Rory?"

Rory froze at the mention of shadows. Seeing the three of them sitting and enjoying their tea with weak sunlight coming through the window, he distinctly noticed the absence of theirs. *No one knows it's missing until they look*, Izzy had said.

How could they not know?

If Rory told them now, would they think he was crazy?

He didn't want to chance it.

"Eel got your tongue?" Miss Cora ventured.

"Oh," Rory said, coming back to himself. "We've just been exploring and stuff. Me and Izzy."

Hilda shook her head. "You two are connected at the hip." She smiled. "I made you some fishcakes. In the kitchen."

Rory went into the kitchen and found two golden brown fishcakes on a small plate. He picked it up and went back to sit on the couch next to his mum.

"Did you hear?" Ox Bells said, waggling his eyebrows at Rory.

"Hear what?" he asked, mouth full.

"The circus has come to Gloom," the former strongman replied. "It's my old troupe. First performance's tonight."

Rory had been so caught up in his own worries he hadn't thought more about the players they had seen. "Oh," he said. "Me and Izzy saw them the other day."

"Where?" Ox Bells asked.

Rory swallowed his fish with a gulp. He didn't have anything to hide, but for some reason, he was hesitant. He didn't want his mum and her friends asking about what he'd been doing or where he'd been going. "Um," he started. "Over by Captain's Quay."

"Captain's Quay?" Miss Cora said sourly. "That's a rough area."

"What were you doing over there?" his mum asked. Her eyes narrowed a bit. Rory knew that look.

"Oh," he said a little too cheerily, "Izzy, you know. She's, um . . . We wanted to . . . There's a shop over there that sells cards and stones and stuff. You know. Fortune-telling."

His mum gave him a skeptical look.

"Fortunes," Ox Bells snorted. "Bunch of rubbish if you ask me. Spirits and such. Humph." He picked up his teacup with huge fingers.

If only you knew, Rory thought. *Not spirits. Shadow stealers. And messages from a goddess. And a boy's heart buried in a back garden.*

"Right." He grinned and feigned laughter. "All a bunch of nonsense."

Rory stuck close to home while Izzy finished her work at Black Maddie's.

There was no real plan, only to arrive at Foxglove Manor under the cover of night and see what they could find out.

His day had been full of errands: filling water bottles from the pump and bringing them inside the house, sweeping out the front room, running to the market to get his mum's order of clams and fish. She was at the tannery and, after morning tea with Ox Bells and Miss Cora, had left Rory with a long list of things to do.

He was happy to work. It kept his mind free of the dark thoughts that had clawed their way to the front of his brain and taken up space.

For a moment, he'd thought of confiding in his mum and her friends. Ox Bells was a big brute. His mum said he knew others just as tough. He could probably kick down the door to the manor and drag Foxglove and Malvonius out by their ears. Rory winced at the painful memory of Malvonius marching him down to Foxglove's cellar.

The cellar.

The double doors with the carving of the woman in the wood.

Mara of the Shadows.

She is the Destroyer. Queen of Sorrow.

Rory shivered, then finished the last of his chores.

CHAPTER TWENTY-FOUR

Masked

The sound of laughter and music grew as Rory and Izzy stepped into Market Square. All of the vendors' stalls had been cleared away to make room for the circus. Torches were staked into the ground, and soft moonlight touched the tops of the surrounding trees, spreading a glow among the festival goers. Several red-and-white tents dotted the space. On any other night, Rory would have admired the beauty of it all. But not tonight. Tonight was different. They were on their way to Foxglove Manor, and Market Square was simply in their path.

"Never seen a real circus before," Izzy admitted.

"Me either," Rory said. "Only in a few books."

"What books?"

"I don't know. Just books."

Ahead of them, on a raised wooden stage, musicians with stringed instruments and drums played a festive tune, the melody drifting up into the night sky. Rory noticed that no one from Gloom danced though.

Izzy looked out at the crowd. "They don't know," she said. "Do they?"

"No," Rory replied. "They don't."

That was all they needed to say. They both knew they were speaking of shadows.

On their right, a man nimbly walked across a cable strung from one makeshift platform to another, his arms spread out for balance. Izzy looked on in wonder. Her red hair was tied up in a knot. Rory knew what that meant. She was ready for a fight again. For a moment, he felt his eyes sting. Her bravery made his stomach pitch. She was the best friend one could ever hope for. He noticed a cloth pouch hanging at her waist.

"What you starin' at?" she said, catching him off guard.

He pointed to the pouch. "What you got in there?"

She turned away from the spectacle and followed Rory's eyes. "Stuff," she said cryptically.

"Uh, what kind of stuff?"

"Stuff that's gonna help us out if we run into trouble."

Rory would have laughed, but he was too anxious. "Do you ever give a straight answer?"

"Depends," Izzy declared.

"Oi! Rory!"

Rory turned to see Ox Bells lumbering up the road. A minute later, he was standing in front of them. Mum's comrade wore a leather vest with no undershirt and pants that ballooned at the very bottom. A forest of thick black hair covered his chest. Rory was reminded of a bear he once saw from a distance when he was exploring in the Glades and way too far from home.

Ox Bells clapped him on the shoulder. He winced.

The big man nodded a greeting. "Rory. Isabella."

Izzy smirked at being called by her proper name. "Aren't you cold?" she asked.

Ox Bells looked at her. "I'm built like a bear," he said, slapping his broad chest. He waved his big hand in the air, grinning. "Sight to behold, innit? This is me old troupe, Rory. Met the new ringmaster the other day. Good fellow. Said he'd decided to come to Gloom to make a little coin." He paused and looked around with admiration at the festivities. "No greater show than the Circus of Fates."

"How long will they be here?" Izzy asked. "And why did you leave the circus, anyway?"

It was a good question, and Rory realized he had never asked it.

Ox Bells twirled one end of his mustache, something he always did when thinking. "Cannonball fell on my head. Knocked me clean out for a week. Never felt right after that."

Rory shot Izzy a glance and tried not to chuckle.

"Back in my day," the former strongman continued, "the Circus of Fates would set up for weeks at a time. Made more money that way." He placed a heavy hand on Rory's shoulder and bent down a little. "Now, if ya wanna see somethin' magnificent, find the mermaid." He finished with a wink.

Izzy rolled her eyes.

Ox Bells rose up and peered into the distance. "Bless my britches. I think I see old One-Handed Nick. Excuse me, if you will."

Rory nodded absently and watched Ox Bells make his way down the road, bellowing a greeting as he did so.

"Maybe Ox Bells could knock down the door to Foxglove

Manor," Izzy suggested, watching his retreating figure, the muscles on his bare arms rippling.

"I thought the same thing," Rory said.

They were interrupted by the arrival of a group of men and women, all dressed in beaded costumes of green, red, and gold, who quickly climbed atop one another, forming a triangle of bodies, the one at the very top standing with hands on hips.

A man on wooden stilts clomped by, his face a mosaic of painted stars. A girl, paper wings spread out behind her, carried a gilded cage holding an exotic bird boasting a spray of blue feathers. Rory's head spun. And then he caught sight of a painted wooden ship held aloft by bare-chested strongmen on either side. At the front of it stood a boy about his age with skin just as dark, but with golden curls on his head.

"Goldenrod," Rory murmured.

And that's when he noticed it.

Torchlight cast the boy's shadow on the cobblestones beneath his feet.

"Izzy," he whisper-shouted. "He has a shadow!"

Izzy watched as the boy who played Goldenrod passed by. Her eyes grew wide. "Look at the others!" she said urgently.

Rory did. Mingled within the crowds of the shadowless

Gloomfolk, he saw that every carnival player had a distinct shadow.

He turned and met Izzy's eyes, which mirrored his own surprise.

"If these people still have shadows . . ." she started.

"That means they can still be stolen," Rory finished.

"Do you think Foxglove knew they were coming to Gloom?" Izzy asked.

"A great harvest is coming," he whispered, as it all clicked into place. "Gloom's shadows weren't enough. They need more. Much more."

A horse galloped by, hooves pounding the cobblestones, its rider sitting high in the saddle. Rory and Izzy jumped out of the way, then moved back toward the edge of the square, where the woods met the town. Trees towered above them, their heavy branches creaking in the wind.

"Could it be?" Izzy asked, looking out at the crowd.

"We have to warn them," Rory said.

"How?" Izzy questioned, turning to face him. "Just go up and tell them they have to leave Gloom or their shadows will get stolen? That's mad, Rory!"

He knew she was right, as usual. The treetops above them continued to creak and groan.

She is coming. I can feel her upon the wind.

"The only thing to do is head to the manor," Izzy declared. "I'll fight Foxglove myself if I have to." She looked at Rory and smiled.

They locked eyes, and Izzy's courage spurred him on. "Right," he said. "Let's do it."

They stepped out of the darkness beneath the trees, ready to face who knew what. Rory was determined to meet it, though, come what may.

A group of jesters wearing brightly colored masks and red robes was approaching. A little girl tugged on one of the jester's sleeves, who then reached down and dropped a treat into the eager child's hand. She turned and ran back toward the crowd, holding aloft her prize as if it were a gold coin.

But something didn't feel right. Rory tensed.

"What are they doing?" Isabella said, backing up. "Why are they walking toward us?"

One of the jesters held up a hand in greeting.

Rory sighed in relief, but as they drew closer, a sense of danger suddenly buzzed around his head. He caught a glimpse of two oddly colored eyes beneath one man's silver mask.

"This way," he said, steering Izzy to the right and toward the crowd. They needed to get closer to the activity before —

But it was too late.

One of the jesters closed the distance between them and grabbed Rory. Strong arms lifted him off his feet.

"Run!" he shouted. "Run, Izzy!"

The other masked attackers surged forward, their robes flapping in the wind. Izzy struck out with her small arms and legs, kicking, scratching, and cursing the whole while, but she was swatted away like a fly. "Help!" she cried out, rising to her feet. "Ox Bells, help!"

But all the music and commotion of the carnival goers drowned out her cries.

Rory struggled, but he was held tight.

"Got you now!" a familiar voice hissed in his ear.

Malvonius.

"No!" Rory shouted. "Ox Bells!"

But no one heard him.

CHAPTER TWENTY-FIVE

Unmasked

Rory struggled against the ropes that bound his wrists.

He was on his knees in Lord Foxglove's cellar.

How they had gotten him there was a mystery. He must have blacked out. The last thing he remembered was a scratchy, smelly bag going over his head and then being carried by two abductors, one at his feet and the other gripping his outstretched, limp arms, like he was a pig headed to slaughter. His head throbbed as if he'd been hit with a rock or a very heavy fist.

His captors stood in a circle around him. Four? Five? He

couldn't tell. His vision was blurry. Was it blood or sweat dripping into his eyes? They still wore jester masks, but Rory was sure that underneath were some of the faces he'd seen the night Foxglove had visitors—the night he'd first heard the words *Arcanus Creatura*.

The familiar dampness brought back memories he wanted to forget—of being marched down to the cellar by his ear and thrown to the icy marble floor.

The figures surrounding him suddenly grew still. A shape appeared out of the shadows at the back of the room. The tall, thin frame could belong to no other.

Foxglove.

But as he drew closer, Rory gasped.

The man he knew as Lord Foxglove was no longer the same.

He had the head of a jackal.

Gold, lustrous fur, slashed with stripes of gray, framed his sharp face. At first Rory thought it was a mask, but when the wild green eyes landed on him, he knew it was no such thing.

Malvonius stepped out of the darkness behind Foxglove and shook his head, a rapid back-and-forth motion that was too fast to comprehend. Rory slowly turned to look, even though he didn't want to.

Where the masked butler had lurked a moment ago stood a man with the head of a hawk, his cruel, yellow beak snapping.

"We meet again," Foxglove said through sharp teeth.

Rory blinked up at them from the floor, hoping it was only a dream.

"You are witnessing something very few will ever see," his former employer went on. "No matter. You won't live to tell anyone." He paused and cocked his jackal head, so unnatural on his human body. Rory felt sick.

"We could eat your cracked bones, but I have another plan for you."

The bones, Rory thought. *Those were human bones on the plates.* His stomach pitched.

His other captors slowly removed their masks. A menagerie of animal features emerged from the darkness: the eyes of an owl; the forked tongue of a snake; the scales of a lizard; the bristling, red comb of a rooster; and the curled horns of a ram. Other aspects blended together, revealing even odder visages: clawed, feathered, and fanged.

It wasn't an illusion. It was real. It was all real.

"We are Arcanus Creatura!" Foxglove cried out. "And I am the Golden Jackal!" A chorus of bestial howls and shrieks went up from the assembled mass.

Rory wanted to clap his hands to his ears but he could not. Sweat poured off him in rivulets.

"We have been blessed," Foxglove said, raising his arms as if addressing Rory as well as his terrible host of creatures. "A gift, we call it, for this is our true form. We are cloaked under her great shadow, which gives us the illusion of humanity."

A wispy trail of smoke appeared in Rory's mind. *Beware, daughter. She is the Destroyer. Queen of Sorrow.*

I thirst. I hunger.

They were doomed.

Lord Foxglove—the Golden Jackal—stepped closer. Rory noticed the man's boots were finely polished, gleaming black and lustrous; he wondered how he could notice such a trivial, pointless detail in the midst of such madness.

He struggled against the tight ropes that bound him and thought of all the things he should have done with his life. He'd never get the chance to learn more about his father from his mum. He wouldn't see Izzy again either—crazy, brave Izzy. His best friend.

And his mum. That hurt most of all. She did everything for him. It was the two of them, together, always looking out for each other.

And now he had failed her. How would she be able to go on?

Rory's head was pounding. All he could do was stare at those black boots of Foxglove's—boots he had polished more than once. *Where is Izzy? She had to have escaped. She'll come for me.* But just as suddenly, another thought occurred to him. *It's not her they want. It's me. The too-curious valet.*

Foxglove took a step closer. "I always knew you were a curious child," he said. "Is that not so?"

Rory didn't answer—couldn't answer.

"But to think that you would seek out one of our disgraced members . . ." Foxglove paused and shook his furred head. "That is the height of insanity."

He's talking about Swoop, Rory realized. *Was the painter one of them? Is that why he knew so much?*

"And now your curiosity has put you in a very tight spot," Foxglove continued. "I believe, when you were galivanting about the manor, you were interested in one particular room, were you not?"

Dread settled over Rory as he remembered the red door and the gruesome light that pulsed along its bottom edge.

"I think you shall see it," Foxglove said. *"Now."*

Rory curled into himself as his captors advanced like something out of a nightmare. Creatures. Secret creatures. Arcanus Creatura.

Long arms and sharp talons reached out for him. He felt

himself go limp. There was no use fighting. The thought of Izzy coming to his rescue faded.

They marched him up the spiral staircase. Rory's legs felt like lead. He wondered if the rest of their bodies took on animal shapes too, or if it was just their heads. He didn't want to know what was under their robes.

They reached the landing. One of the beasts steered him forward with strong hands that pinched his shoulders. *The armor,* Rory thought with a glimmer of hope. *It's right around the corner at the end of the hall. The lance. A weapon.*

His small moment of hope disappeared as they stopped in front of the red door.

"Unbind him," Foxglove said. "He must kneel before our queen and lay out his hands in supplication."

Rory wasn't sure what that meant, but the creature behind him cut his ropes. Hot breath steamed against the back of his neck, but his hands were free.

I can make a run for it. Grab the lance and . . .

Foxglove reached into the folds of his clothing and withdrew a strange, elaborate key with a sharp point at its end.

Rory closed and then opened his eyes again. The key wasn't just a strange shape—it seemed to be made of something unnatural. Black wisps swirled around it and caressed

Foxglove's hand. *A shadow key?* Rory wondered. But before he could think on it any longer, Foxglove spoke again.

"You will see her now. Our glorious queen. In all her eternal magnificence." He gave Rory a gloating, jackal-faced smile.

Boom.

A deafening crash.

Rory turned. Desperate. Hoping.

Foxglove and his minions rushed down the corridor and around the corner, into the main hall.

Rory stood up quickly and followed.

He grabbed the lance from the knight's hand and peered down the hall.

Izzy, Ox Bells, and another man with a hook for a hand stood among the ruins of the front door, now in splinters.

"Oi!" Ox Bells shouted. "What in the name of the sea gods?"

Izzy, Ox Bells, and the other man, who had to be Ox Bells's friend One-Handed Nick, charged down the hall and tore into the monstrous creatures, who fell upon them in a rush of howls and screams.

"Run, lad!" Ox Bells cried, as he blocked a blow from hawk-faced Malvonius. "Take Izzy and go!"

"No!" Izzy shot back, and just as she did when she saved

Rory from the Canaries, she strung together a flurry of unfamiliar words, but this time, she clapped her small hands together. A flash of white smoke erupted in the air.

Rory didn't know where to direct his attention in the midst of all the chaos. He swung the long lance in an arc, sending a bull-headed creature smashing into the wall. Glass and gold frames crashed to the floor.

Ox Bells and One-Handed Nick seemed to be getting the best of Foxglove and Arcanus Creatura. Rory watched as his mum's friend punched and kicked his abductors to the floor. A few already lay seemingly lifeless, blood streaming from their animal faces.

In that moment, Rory made a decision. He knew he wasn't a fighter, but he had to be brave. He had to help.

He rushed at Foxglove with the lance, charging straight at him. The Golden Jackal snarled and stepped aside, easily dodging the attack. Rory turned around and faced the creature again. The fighting raged everywhere, but for a moment, it seemed as if it were just the two of them.

"Rory!" Izzy shouted, and ran up alongside him.

Foxglove cocked his strange head again. "Pretty thing."

"Shut up, you freak!" she cried, and tucked her chin and ran forward, knocking her small head into his midsection.

Foxglove fell, and Rory dropped his lance and dove onto him.

Izzy scrambled away, pulling the whalebone dagger from the pouch at her side. She rushed back and stood over Foxglove as Rory put his hands around the Golden Jackal's throat. He was going to choke the life out of him. The strange sensation of fur on Rory's skin felt wrong. He couldn't do this. It was like killing an animal.

"We know what you've done!" Izzy shouted. "With our shadows!"

"And with the boy," Rory said, using all the weight of his body to hold Foxglove down. "Timothy. You killed him!"

Izzy knelt and raised the dagger over Foxglove's chest.

She could do it, Rory thought, remembering the last time he'd seen that knife, when Izzy had thought her prospective customer was an enemy. *She could do it in an instant.*

Rory's hands tightened around Foxglove's throat.

No, a quiet voice sounded in his head. They were taking him to see their queen, Foxglove had said. She was the one he and Izzy had to stop — Mara of the Shadows.

He jumped up.

Foxglove immediately began to cough and sputter.

"What are you doing?" Izzy shouted. "We have to stop him!"

The fighting around them had ceased. Foxglove's pack of creatures lay crumpled in the hallway, some barely moving and others not moving at all.

Ox Bells picked himself up from the floor. A gruesome gash ran along his neck. One-Handed Nick was nowhere to be seen.

"The room with the red door," Rory sputtered, out of breath. "That's where they were taking me. That's where she is—Mara of the Shadows. We have to stop *her.*"

"You will die," a trembling voice whispered.

Rory turned.

Foxglove was holding himself up by resting one out-stretched arm against the wall, while the other gently caressed the fur at his throat. "Your shadow has been ripped from your body, child. Never to return."

"Kill him, Rory," Izzy said. "If you don't, I will."

Rory looked to his friend, and then back to Foxglove.

"You will burn in her fire," Foxglove croaked, his jackal teeth stained with blood. "She thirsts. She hungers." He slumped to the floor.

Rory felt nothing. He wasn't sure if Foxglove was dead or not, but he didn't have the slightest bit of compassion.

"Rory," Ox Bells called out from behind them, stum-bling a bit, then opening and closing his eyes as if dizzy.

"Isabella . . . what the—?" He crashed to the floor, scattering splintered frames beneath him.

It took all of Rory's and Izzy's strength to drag Ox Bells outside. They propped him up against the broken door frame as the strongman mumbled and groaned.

"Where's your friend?" Rory asked.

"One-Handed Nick," Izzy added.

A purplish-black bruise bloomed under Ox Bell's left eye. "Creatures," he said. "Tears of a . . ." His head slumped to his chest.

Izzy knelt, then picked up Ox Bell's huge hand and felt his pulse. She closed her eyes and moved her lips, counting silently, then stood back up. "He'll be okay," she said.

"What about Nick?" Rory asked.

"I don't know where he is," Izzy said, peering around the shadowy front yard.

They stepped back through the broken remains of the door. The sound of lumbering feet made them both turn.

One-Handed Nick staggered out of the drawing room, his face bruised and his expression dazed. "Great winds," he said. "Where the hell am I?"

"Ox Bells is outside," Izzy said, angling her head down the hall. "Take care of him."

Nick nodded and stumbled past them. "Monsters," he muttered. "Well, I never . . . clams and oysters."

Rory turned to his friend. "I'm going through that red door, Izzy. I don't know what I'll find, but I'm seeing this through."

Izzy took his hand in hers. "Not without me, you aren't."

And together, they rushed down the hall.

CHAPTER TWENTY-SIX

The Infernal Machine

The shadow key lay at Rory's feet. Black tendrils swirled around it. "Foxglove was about to use that to open the door," he said.

Izzy bent and looked more closely. "Don't touch it," she warned, rising back up.

Rory lifted his head and focused on the red door. The thin, spidery trees moved in a breeze he couldn't feel. "We have to go through," he said. "We have to face her."

"Mara," Izzy whispered.

Rory bent down and put his fingers around the key. Izzy sucked in a breath.

The key felt solid, although the smoky lines that licked Rory's hand did not.

"Open the door," Izzy urged. "Quickly!"

Rory put the key into the lock.

He turned it.

He heard a distinct *click,* as he had when he'd spied on Malvonius and Foxglove during his first days at the manor. He pushed the door open.

"Great winds," Izzy said quietly.

Directly in front of them stood a tall tree with gnarled roots and drooping black leaves. Rory stepped forward and laid his hand on the rough bark. "Izzy?" he asked. "Where are we?"

"I don't know," she answered.

A dense forest lay beyond the tree.

Rory turned around. Behind them, only shadows loomed.

He spun around to face the forest again, and felt cool air on his face. "We're outside," he said. "How can we be outside?"

A dim red light played at the edges of their vision, but there was no sign of its source. Rory thought of the red glow he'd seen pulsing at the door's bottom edge.

"They were creatures," Izzy said in disbelief. "Not human, Rory. *Creatures.*"

"I know," he said. "You were right, when I first asked you what *Arcanus Creatura* meant—secret creatures."

Izzy shook her head. "But why animals? I don't understand. I thought they were shadow stealers."

"I don't know what they are," Rory replied, remembering the weird sensation of fur in his hands as he had tried to strangle Foxglove.

Izzy cupped her hands to her mouth. "Hello?" she called.

"Shhh," Rory whispered. "We have no idea where we are or . . . who's in here."

"*She's* in here," Izzy said, fear creeping into her voice. "Mara of the Shadows."

Rory shivered at the name spoken aloud. "I knew it was all tied together," he said, peering around as he walked. "She's their leader. Foxglove called her 'our glorious queen.'"

"His queen?" Izzy echoed. "Do you think he *made* Swoop paint that picture, and then Swoop covered it up because he was afraid of it?"

"Foxglove said Swoop was a member of Arcanus Creatura," Rory replied. "A *former* member."

Izzy shook her head. "I knew that weasel was up to no good."

The loamy smell of upturned earth and dampness filled Rory's nostrils. He looked around. "Let's walk, and see what we can find."

They set out hesitantly, one wary step at a time. The red light faded, leaving only a dim grayness. Overhead, the dark clouds seemed ready to smother them. Rory felt a tightness in his chest. They tried to walk quietly, but branches snapped under their feet. Rory didn't want to speak again, for fear of being heard.

"There's a path." Izzy pointed to the left. "This way."

She turned and Rory followed, his mind still on the fight at the manor. The knight's lance—he had forgotten it. He was about to curse himself when he suddenly remembered he had his own dagger and slipped it out of his boot. He hadn't even thought to use it when he had been in the cellar, held as a prisoner. It turned out that fighting enemies didn't always happen the way it did in books. It was much more frightening and frantic.

The path they walked on was littered with dead, black leaves. Rory heard his heartbeat thrumming in his ears.

"What are we going to do if we find . . . her?" Izzy whispered, finally breaking the eerie silence.

Rory was relieved to hear her voice, but he didn't have an answer. It was as if he was asleep and awake at the same time. He shrugged, uncertain how to respond. Izzy seemed to understand and pressed no further.

They walked on. The landscape didn't change, but Rory started to feel as if a fog was descending. He felt it on his skin first, and then he saw it—a thin layer of black soot, which he brushed off his arm.

"It's on me too," Izzy complained.

He was about to reply when they came around a bend in the trail and stopped in their tracks.

A few steps ahead of them sat what looked to be a massive iron forge. Four thick legs supported its weight, ending in clawed feet. Its gaping mouth was nothing but darkness, releasing wispy trails of black and red smoke that swirled up to become lost in the tree branches and shadows above.

"Tears of a fish," Izzy whispered.

Rory remembered the hissing sound he'd heard coming from the red door before. Now he knew its source. He gripped his dagger tightly in his sweating fist.

"What do we do?" asked Izzy doubtfully.

As if in answer, black mist began to pour out of the forge. And then, out of the forge's mouth, two shadow hands gripped the sides and something began to pull itself free.

Izzy and Rory gasped.

The formless black mass in front of them had red at its

very center, just as Rory had seen in his dreams. As they watched, both of them crouched, ready to flee or fight—they weren't sure which—the shape began to reveal itself.

It was a woman.

She was at least six feet tall, with skin as white as milk. Wispy, black threads swirled around her insubstantial form. Rory wasn't sure if she was wearing clothes or cloaked only in shadows. Her hair was a tangle of leaves and vines.

He felt woozy, like he was about to faint. Sweat beaded on his forehead. The woman's eyes landed on him.

"Where are my beasts?" she asked.

The voice that came out of her was unusually deep, but also melodious, as if it could lull one to sleep.

Rory gave Izzy a shaky, sidelong glance.

The woman took a step forward. Rory felt heat coming off her, as if she were made of fire. Her cold, vacant eyes pierced his soul.

"Are you disciples of mine?" she asked.

Rory could have shaken his head no, but he remained still.

"Tell the jackal I am waiting," she said testily. "How many more do I need before I am whole again?"

Rory swallowed.

We will need more. Much more.

Izzy remained just as still as Rory. The air felt cooler, as if icy fingers were reaching out to touch them.

"My wounds are many," the woman said. "I thirst. I hunger."

Rory swallowed hard.

Foxglove's queen stared at both of them with an imperious gaze. "Speak, humans!"

The dizziness in Rory's head disappeared and was replaced by a dull ache. "We know what you're doing," he said quickly. "Stealing shadows."

"We're here to stop you," Izzy added.

The woman tilted her head, revealing a long, snake-like neck. "So you are *not* my acolytes."

Rory swallowed again. "Who are you?" he managed to ask.

But he already knew. He'd seen her likeness carved into Foxglove's cellar door and painted on Swoop's wall.

Mara of the Shadows. Queen of Sorrow.

The woman drew her head back as if insulted. "Stupid children!" she spat out, and raised her head higher. For a moment, she seemed to grow as tall as the trees around her. "I have many names," she said slowly, beginning to walk toward them.

Izzy and Rory backed up again.

"Prosperine," the woman said. "Lamia. Jezebeth. I am all of these. But now, I am Mara. And you should be kneeling."

Rory still held the dagger tightly, but he had no idea what, if anything, it could do against such a strange foe.

Mara's empty eyes roamed over them. "I see that you two have already been excised," she snapped. "If not, I would draw your shadows out slowly, so you could feel the pain."

"You don't scare us," Izzy proclaimed. Rory tried to appear just as brave, but he knew his face betrayed him.

Mara threw her head back and laughed, and her hair writhed like a bouquet of snakes. Her mouth was full of sharp, black teeth.

She cocked her head again. "Where do you come from, boy? You have a dark look about you. A look I have seen before."

Rory's tongue felt heavy. He and Izzy had been brave enough to enter, but they had no plan of attack. Nothing.

Mara looked beyond them, into the thick forest of trees with black, drooping leaves. "The world exists in shadow," she said softly. "You only see a half world. I see all." She paused, considering them. "Before I kill you, can you tell me where my beasts are? I would assume they are not far."

She was going to kill them. Rory realized he had to act fast. He had to do something. Anything.

He took a step forward, the dagger gripped in his sweating fist. Izzy stood ready beside him.

"Oh my," Mara scoffed. "Are all humans so brave?"

"If we have to be," Izzy shot back.

Mara raised her hand in the air and twitched her fingers in an intricate motion. "Enough."

Curls of black smoke trailed from her fingertips and coiled around Izzy's throat.

"No!" Izzy cried out, struggling to move her arms, which had become pinned to her sides by more smoke-like coils.

As Rory reached out to help, Mara flicked her hands again, sending more shadow ropes that snaked around his midsection. The dagger fell from his hand. He fought to move but could only twist to-and-fro, barely keeping his balance.

The coil began to rise, working its way up his torso. He was going to be strangled, he realized, and so was Izzy.

A sort of calmness washed over him at that moment. This was it. He and Izzy should have known better than to get into something they didn't understand.

But he was too curious, like Foxglove had said. A stupid,

curious boy, and now he and Izzy would pay for it—with their lives.

"Help," Izzy croaked out, her face turning a shade of purplish red Rory had never seen before. Tears streamed down her cheeks. But he could not help her. He couldn't even help himself.

The black vines were winding their way up his neck. Mara watched them both with grim fascination, her mouth opening and closing silently in some sort of weird delight. "My beasts have been busy," she said, "feeding me shadows. Do you know why I call them that? Beasts?"

Rory couldn't answer.

"They're my pets, really," the Queen of Sorrow boasted. "I made them that way. I fancied certain creatures, you see, and my disciples were eager to please. So I . . . *transformed* them."

Rory wondered what kind of dark magic could do such a thing.

"But I still give them the illusion of humanity," the terrible queen continued, "so they may serve me in your mortal world."

Rory wriggled more, but to no avail. Izzy's eyes were closed now, as if she had accepted her fate. She swayed like a top winding down, ready to fall at any moment.

Mara glanced over her shoulder at the forge and then turned back around to face them. "Only a few more shadows for the Infernal Machine and I will fully walk in this world once again."

Infernal Machine? Rory thought. *Is that what that thing is?*

Not too much longer now and it would be over. He closed his eyes.

Izzy crashed to the ground.

Suddenly, a wellspring of strength rose up in Rory. Izzy was his best friend, and all she'd ever wanted to do was help him. He couldn't let her die.

"No!"

It wasn't a scream. It was a shout, propelled by something buried deep down inside of him. He felt it coursing through his body, running through his arms and legs. Maybe Izzy was right — maybe he did have a special power to call upon.

He focused on it. It was a pulse, pounding in his temples. *Boom, boom, boom.* He pushed his will as hard as he could. *"Stop!"*

The ropelike bonds that held him snapped loose.

His hands flew to his throat. In his rush to breathe, he grasped the chain around his neck and yanked, sending the black stone he wore to the ground, where it shattered on a rock.

He reached out to Izzy, but his hands found no purchase on the shadow ropes, which dissolved into thin tendrils when he touched them.

Izzy gasped and opened her eyes.

Rory retrieved his dagger from the ground, ready to take his last stand. But Mara's attention was drawn elsewhere.

She was focused on something at Rory's feet—completely unconcerned, it seemed, that her captives were suddenly free. "What . . . is that?" she asked, as if annoyed.

Rory looked at the shards of the onyx below him.

A wispy thread of black leaked from the broken pieces.

Mara tilted her head, watching.

The thread of black grew in a spiral that rose from the stone, taking on a shape. A human shape.

Mara approached slowly, fascinated. "That . . . What is that?"

Rory didn't answer. He had no idea. But as Izzy finally regained her breath beside him, the form grew taller. More solid. It was a black silhouette, and it bore a distinct profile.

"It can't be," Rory whispered.

In a blur of motion, the thing's shadowy arm reached out and snatched the dagger from Rory's hand.

Izzy grabbed Rory and pulled him back.

The queen rose up to her full height and, with her long neck outstretched, opened her mouth wide. A cloud of spiders poured forth, and a poisonous stench filled the air.

Rory and Izzy coughed and backed away even farther, against the broad trunk of a tree. The shadow spiders scattered and raced toward them, running up their ankles and into the crevices of their clothes.

"No!" Izzy screamed, slapping the terrible things away.

Rory frantically did the same. They were a wave, a tide of biting, scuttling creatures. He danced around, trying to get them off while still trying to keep an eye on Mara.

The shadowy figure that had emerged from the onyx stalked its prey, a silky blur of rippling motion. The spiders seemed to avoid it, and continued their assault.

Izzy reached into the pouch at her side with trembling fingers. "Spiders, spiders, bite no more! Begone at once and forevermore!"

She cupped her hand to her mouth and blew, releasing a cloud of white mist.

The spiders fell to the ground, thousands of them, and then fled for the surrounding trees.

Mara cursed and drew herself up again to blow out another breath. But in one quick motion, the shadow thing stepped aside, tossed the dagger to its other hand, crouched, and plunged the blade into the queen's shadowy robes.

The forest flashed red and then back to dreary gray as a piercing scream echoed in Rory's ears. He grabbed Izzy's hand and clenched it tightly.

Thousands of black tendrils floated away from Mara's body as her form disappeared in a burst of black smoke. A disembodied scream rang out again, and then there was silence.

Rory heard Izzy's shallow breaths matching his own.

"Is she . . . gone?" she asked cautiously.

Rory didn't answer.

The shadow figure turned to face them. Its shoulders rose and fell, as if winded.

And then it charged straight at him.

CHAPTER TWENTY-SEVEN

The Valet Finds That
Which Was Lost

Rory crashed to the ground.

Suffocating pressure hit him square in the chest, knocking the wind out of him.

Izzy knelt and helped him up. The shadow figure was nowhere to be seen.

Rory rose unsteadily and laid a hand on his heart. "Something's . . . different," he said.

Izzy rubbed her throat. Then she froze and slowly drew her hand away from her neck. She pointed. "Look."

Rory followed her finger. The gray sky overhead was

lighter now, and a glint of sunlight shone onto the forest floor.

Rory froze, speechless. He moved his arm, and his shadow returned the gesture. He lifted his arm, then waved his hand in the air. "My shadow," he said. "Right there."

Izzy stared in disbelief.

"It came from you," she said. "I mean, it came out of the stone you wear. How?"

"I don't know," Rory answered.

He scanned the ground, looking for the broken shards of onyx, but there was nothing to be found.

The forge—the Infernal Machine—began to hiss again, and they both tensed, then watched as a torrent of shadowy figures poured forth from it. They took on human shapes, just like the one from Rory's stone.

Then they drifted to the trees and spread out, floating back the way Rory and Izzy had come.

"Are the shadows," Izzy began, " . . . returning?"

"Can it really be?" Rory asked hopefully.

Izzy jumped back as a dark figure rushed toward her.

"No!" she cried out, putting up her hands in a defensive gesture as she was knocked to the ground.

"Izzy!" Rory shouted, dropping to his knees and taking her hand.

He watched as the shadow seeped into her, like water being absorbed by a sponge.

She lay there a moment, breathing hard, her eyes wide with alarm. "I think I'm okay," she said.

Rory guided her up by her elbow. He examined her face for any sign of injury.

Izzy breathed out. "I'm okay," she said again. She touched her chest. "I feel it too. Spreading through me. It's my shadow, Rory!" She looked to the patch of sun and waved her hand back and forth. "I see it! Hello, shadow!"

Rory almost laughed. "Unbelievable," he whispered. His hand instinctively went to the stone around his neck, but found nothing there to touch.

He breathed out through his nostrils.

Izzy spun in a circle, then threw her arms over her head. Her shadow did the same.

Rory watched his friend revel in the moment, but they weren't done yet.

Izzy stopped spinning. They paused for a moment as the reality of the situation came back to them.

"We have to get out of here," she said, and cocked her head toward the way they'd come.

Rory nodded, still taking everything in. *My shadow was in the stone? How?*

"Let's try to find the way back," he said, turning around.

"It can't be that hard," Izzy declared.

They began to walk. Rays of sunlight shone down through skeletal bare trees—all the black leaves had fallen from their thin branches.

"What is this place anyway?" Izzy asked.

"I don't know," Rory replied. "Someplace she fed on shadows. With that . . . *machine*, she called it. The Infernal Machine." He shook his head, relieved that it was over.

Izzy nodded thoughtfully. "And now the shadows have returned."

"Let's hope," Rory countered, thinking of his mum and everyone else in Gloom. *Sea Bell*, he reminded himself.

A flock of crows exploded from a stand of trees. They both jumped, startled, and as they watched, the crows soared upward, and then fell back to earth in heaps of ash.

They stepped cautiously around the remains. "Weird," Rory muttered.

"Let's go faster," Izzy urged. "This place gives me the creeps."

They continued along the path. Every now and then, Rory caught a glimpse of his shadow. *The stone*, he mused again. *How?*

"She called them her creatures," Izzy said. "Foxglove and Malvonius. Her beasts."

Rory recalled the bird face he'd seen when he'd come upon the butler unawares. "Who would let someone do that to them?" he questioned. "To be . . . changed like that?"

"Evil people," Izzy replied.

Rory nodded. He didn't want to think about it anymore. He just wanted to go home.

The trees became sparser as they continued walking. Rory breathed in deeply. The air was fresh and the sky overhead was a color he hadn't seen very often — blue, with white clouds.

"Look," Izzy said, pointing.

Up ahead, the red door was open. Shadows stirred beyond it.

"So strange," Izzy whispered.

Rory led the way forward. "It's where we came in," he said. "Let's hope the house is on the other side."

Izzy peered around. "And not some other weird place like this."

When they walked through the open door, Rory sighed a breath of relief. The familiar rose-colored walls were a comfort to see.

Izzy pulled the door shut, leaving behind whatever other mysteries the black forest held.

Inside, all was quiet. Rory and Izzy peered around warily. There was no sign of Foxglove, or of Mara's other beasts.

The long hall was empty, but for the splintered and smashed portraits that had fallen in the melee. Rory saw the painting of Foxglove and shook his head.

"What is this?" Izzy called. Her head was bowed, studying something on the floor. Rory stepped up alongside her. Mounds of black ash were spread about. He raised his head and looked to the spot where he'd last seen Foxglove—the Golden Jackal—leaning up against the wall, winded. The only thing there was another pile of ash.

Izzy bent down, reaching out a hand.

"Don't!" Rory shouted, grabbing her arm. "We don't know what it could do to us. Don't touch it."

"Disgusting," Izzy said, turning up her nose and straightening again.

"It's them," Rory said. "Foxglove and the others. When their queen died, maybe they died with her."

"Just like those birds we saw," Izzy replied. "They turned to ash too."

They tensed at the sound of heavy footsteps.

"Rory?" a deep voice called. "Isabella?"

Ox Bells and One-Handed Nick came down the stairs at the end of the hall. As they drew closer, Rory saw that both men still looked dazed.

Ox Bells stopped in front of them. He stared at Rory and Izzy for a long moment.

"What in the world did you get yourself into, Rory?" he finally asked.

Rory led the way out of Foxglove Manor. The crisp air on his face was refreshing.

"Where were you two?" Ox Bells asked, a hint of anger in his voice. "I know you dragged me outside. We searched this house high and low! Where in the name of the blasted—"

"There was still something we had to do," Izzy said, cutting him off.

Ox Bells shook his massive head, confounded.

"You and Vincent were right," Rory said. "There *was* something evil in that house."

"They had animal faces," One-Handed Nick said. "I've seen my fair share of strangeness in this world, but ... nothing like that."

Rory opened his mouth to explain, but then thought better of it. *There'll be plenty of time for answers.* Enough was enough for now.

"Funny thing," Ox Bells said. "Not long after we bested those . . . creatures, I felt something strike me in the chest. 'Twas like thunder."

"And then a bit of calm," Nick said. "Like a peacefulness spreading through me, if you take my meaning."

Rory and Izzy looked at each other and grinned. They dropped back a little and let Ox Bells lead the way.

"I wasn't going to let them take you," Izzy whispered to Rory as they continued to walk. "I found Ox Bells right away and we came as fast as we could."

"I'm glad you did," Rory said, then paused. He lowered his voice. "What did you do? With the white smoke? The spiders?"

Izzy smiled proudly. "It was one of the first spells my mum ever taught me."

"Really?"

"Yeah. She uses it to keep spiders out of the house."

Rory felt a funny sensation in his stomach, which seemed to work its way up to his face. He opened his mouth and a sound came out. It was laughter.

Ox Bells turned around and looked at them askance. "What's wrong with you two? You in shock?"

Rory looked to Izzy.

And then they started laughing again.

"Kids." Ox Bells smirked. "Little otters."

CHAPTER TWENTY-EIGHT

Neither Sloop, Nor Jackdaw

Although several weeks had passed, the defeat of Mara of the Shadows was still fresh in Rory's memory, like a lingering dream he wanted to forget.

But he couldn't.

Nightmares plagued him — visions of creeping shadows and blood-red forests; the wild, animal faces of Lord Foxglove and Malvonius. His mum woke him on many occasions, soothing his forehead with a cool hand and whispering words of comfort.

Rory hadn't wanted to worry her, so he hadn't told her

about all of the madness that had been going on in Gloom. It was Ox Bells who'd done that.

At first, Rory was angry with him, but soon he understood that keeping it from his mum would have been a terrible mistake, something that would have haunted him for the rest of his days.

It turned out she was mostly just concerned for his safety, and Izzy's. "You could have told me all of this!" She'd fumed. "We could have rallied together! All of us — shirrifs, Ox Bells and his friends, even Izzy's mum! She . . . knows some things. At least that's what I've heard."

After that, Rory was ashamed that he'd kept things from his mum. She was a brave woman, and would have fought to protect the people she loved.

Rory often caught her looking at her own shadow and shaking her head, as if she still couldn't believe that it was all true.

He couldn't believe it either — his own shadow, coming to defend him. He didn't know if he ever really would.

Rory and Izzy sat on the docks of Quintus Harbor. The sound of water slapping the pilings provided a steady rhythm.

"I never knew something so strange could happen here," Rory said softly, almost to himself.

"But it did," Izzy replied. "And we actually saved people, Rory. We *saved* them!"

She was right, he knew. They had helped release the shadows trapped in what Mara called the Infernal Machine. Now they were back with the people who had lost them.

The Circus of Fates, the carnival, was still entertaining the townspeople. Rory and Izzy had visited often, walking among the crowds of smiling and laughing people. Rory had never seen so many happy faces in Gloom before.

But they didn't even know, he mused. Didn't know that their shadows had been stolen and used to feed an evil queen.

Maybe, he thought, as he looked out over the water, *they had sensed that something had returned to their bodies, like Ox Bells and One-Handed Nick had.* Their *essence,* Swoop called it.

But did this mean their shadows were tainted now? Was there a piece of darkness lingering in them all, ready to take on another shape?

Rory shuddered and pushed the thought away.

Small boats rocked gently on the water, their sails snapping in the breeze. Farther out, a massive ship with white sails as large as clouds moved with a speed that betrayed its size. The sun shot down in brilliant rays, casting Rory's shadow alongside him.

"There are still things I wonder about," he said.

A gray seagull landed next to him and flew away quickly, squawking and flapping its wings, a crumb of bread dangling from its beak.

"Like what?"

He shifted on the hard planks, then dug his finger into a crack in a slat of wood. "Like why I dreamed about . . ." He still didn't feel comfortable saying the name, although he knew the threat was gone—at least he had hoped so. "Her," he finished.

Izzy lazily swung her legs back and forth over the edge of the dock. "I still think you've got some kind of magic," she said. "The carved deck says we live many lives and that, when we die, we carry our stuff over from the last one."

"What 'stuff'?" Rory asked.

Izzy shrugged. "Dunno. Our brains?"

Rory chuckled and looked back toward the water. "And the stone that was my father's. I don't understand that either. How did it . . ." He trailed off.

Izzy only shook her head.

Rory turned at the sound of voices coming from farther down the dock. A few people were congregating at its very end. "What's going on down there?" he asked, pointing.

"Let's go see."

The crowd was growing. Men, women, and children were all talking in an excited babble of voices and looking out toward the water, pointing into the distance.

"Never seen a ship that big before."

"It's a sloop."

"It's not a sloop. It's a jackdaw."

Rory shaded his eyes with the edge of his hand. The massive ship he had spotted moments ago was closer now, parting the water before it, coming in from the Black Sea, which Quintus Harbor fed into. It was the largest ship he'd ever seen as well.

It had two masts—the tallest of which, called the main, rose into the air higher than several lampposts linked together. It carried two sails, one square and the other triangular. The other mast had smaller sails with staysails in between.

"I tell you, it's a jackdaw," another voice rang out.

"I know a sloop when I see one, you ninny."

But Rory knew they were both wrong.

He had read books about the sea and was quite familiar with the big ships that were in all the stories.

It was a brigantine, the largest and fastest sailing vessel known to man. As it drew closer, he saw small figures preparing the ship to dock. The crew eased off the mainsheet to slow its approach. A small figure grabbed the boom and pushed it back hard against the wind. Rory watched in admiration. He'd only read about these things in books. To see it actually happening right in front of him filled his heart with excitement.

As the ship drifted between two pilings—the widest in Quintus Harbor—Rory looked on in awe. From the prow, a golden mermaid figurehead stared out at him.

"What in the world?" Izzy exclaimed. "What's a ship like that doing in Gloom?"

But Rory didn't answer. He was looking at the crew as they threw heavy chains onto the dock. A few wind-bitten Gloom sailors tied the chains to cleats.

Rory knew where the captain's quarters were. They were right at the stern of the ship, and it was the captain whom he wanted to see.

The crowd hushed. The crew assembled on the deck in a sort of square formation and drew themselves to attention. Rory looked at their faces. They were all dark skinned— some like him and others baked by the heat of the sun. The women looked just as fierce as the men.

The crowd waited.

And then, a man emerged from the captain's quarters.

His skin was like ebony. He carried a rough-hewn

wooden staff, almost as tall as he was. Rory took note of the muscles in his arms, like cords of rope. His hair was golden and tied into a topknot, something Rory had never seen on a man before. He wore a weather-stained vest, loose-fitting trousers, and leather sandals tied around his ankles.

Izzy stuck an elbow into Rory's side. "Is that . . . ?" she whispered, her eyes wide. "It can't be."

"It is," Rory said. "That has to be Goldenrod."

Without any kind of command that Rory could see or hear, several of the crew went to the starboard side of the ship and used ropes to lower a wooden plank dockside. Rory noticed the decorative handrails, but the captain didn't reach out to steady himself, only walked with a sense of purpose unlike any Rory had ever seen. Silence filled the air, broken only by the gulls calling overhead. The man came around to stand at the front of his ship. "It's been many a year since I was last in this town," he said, and his rich, deep voice carried out over the assembled mass. He looked from left to right, seeming to study the face of every person there. "Does Black Maddie's still stand? My crew and I could do with a good meal and a dry bed."

"Aye," a bearded old man called out. "Hasn't changed much. Still beer and fish every day."

A few chuckles sounded in the crowd. Rory jumped as

someone behind him laid their hands on his shoulders. He turned around quickly.

His mum stared at him. "Vincent said there was something happening down here," she said excitedly and in a low voice. "Something I wouldn't want to miss."

Rory turned back around. The captain's attention had been drawn away from the onlookers. He was staring at Rory's mum. "Hilda?"

Rory and Izzy looked at each other, confused.

Hilda cocked her head and furrowed her brow. Suddenly, her grip on Rory's shoulders tightened. "By the sea gods," she whispered.

"Mum?" Rory asked, turning to face her again, completely taken aback. "What's going on?"

Hilda Sorenson blew out a trembling breath. "Rory," she said, "that man is your father."

CHAPTER TWENTY-NINE

Tales from the Sea

They sat together in the small kitchen. Fish stew simmered in an iron pot on the stove, sending the aroma of paprika, onion, and black pepper around the room. On any other day, Rory's mouth would have been watering, and he'd have been eager to fill himself a bowl. But not today. Myth had turned into reality. He was stunned. Flabbergasted. The man sitting across from him was his father. *His father.*

"You're *real?*" asked Izzy, who hadn't taken her eyes off the strange man yet.

He smiled grimly. "As real as you, girl."

"Izzy," she said, with a little bow of her head. "My name's Izzy . . . sir."

"*Izzy*," he murmured, as if he were trying out the name for size. "Yes, Izzy. I am the one they call Goldenrod, but I'm afraid the tales of my adventures have been told so many times they no longer bear the ring of truth."

Hilda Sorenson rested her elbows on the table and laced her fingers together. "I thought you were dead," she said, an edge to her voice. "I told Rory that you drowned at sea. And now you come back, calling yourself Goldenrod?" She shook her head.

"I did not give myself the name," Rory's father said, a note of contrition in his voice. "It was given to me by . . ." he paused, "others."

Rory stared down at the stained wooden table. He bit his lip. He didn't know what to say. The father he never knew was suddenly sitting right next to him. Not just his father. A legend. A myth.

Rory raised his head. His father had dark, almond-shaped eyes, just like his son, and a scar on his left cheek. They had the same nose, too—somewhat sharp with a little bump in the middle. Rory'd thought he'd gotten the bump when he had fallen out of a tree at six years old. But now he knew the truth. It was something that had been passed on, from father to son.

"I was gone for many a year," the mariner said. "And for that, Hilda, I beg your forgiveness." He turned to Rory. "Your mother didn't know I still lived. I have been . . ." He paused again, as if at a loss for words. "There is much I must tell you."

He lifted a mug of water and took a long drink. The room was still. Not even the creak of a chair could be heard. Goldenrod set the mug back onto the table. He rubbed his knuckles, which Rory noticed were badly scarred. "Many years ago, before you were born, Rory, I was a mariner for the Yellow Trident Sea Company. I traveled far and wide, to distant lands uncharted by any map."

"Did you ride a seahorse?" Izzy asked, wide-eyed. "That's what the stories say. That you tamed a wild seahorse and made it your steed."

Goldenrod smiled, and the lines around his eyes crinkled. "Tell me . . . Izzy. If I had a seahorse, wouldn't I have to breathe underwater?"

Izzy screwed up her face. "I guess so," she said, deflated, and then: "Or not?"

Rory almost chuckled.

"No," Goldenrod said. "In all my travels, I have never

found a seahorse big enough to ride." He looked at Rory's mum for a long moment. "But I did find a woman I fell in love with — in a small, odd little town — and she was as beautiful as the sea itself."

Rory's ears burned. He felt like he'd just heard something private. He glanced at Izzy, who seemed to be thinking the same thing.

Hilda Sorenson remained stoic.

"But I was called away," Goldenrod said. "It was my duty. I had to leave the Yellow Trident." He studied the table. When he looked up, Rory saw his eyes sparkle. "I've walked the red sands of Amerand, met the Chevalier of Mercia, and dined on pomegranates with the Emperor of Asiata. I've sailed to an island in the Black Sea called Quis, where the only form of life is a species of bird with wings of fire."

Rory was swept away as his father's deep and resonant voice reverberated in the room.

"What happened to your hair?" Hilda asked, unimpressed. "When you left all those years ago, it was as black as coal."

Goldenrod leaned back from the table and released a sigh. "The bane of my existence," he said, almost in embarrassment, it seemed to Rory.

"Soon after I left Gloom, my crew docked in a place called Otak. There are enchanters in that city who say they can read the future. Over a blazing fire of purple flames, one of them told me I was destined for great things, and that I should have a name worthy of remembrance. He said I would be called 'Goldenrod.' When I awoke the next morning . . ."

He ran a finger through a loose strand of golden hair and then raised his eyebrows.

"Your hair changed color overnight?" Rory asked, amazed.

His father only nodded. "From that day forward, in every town, hamlet, village, and city I left, people spoke of the Black Mariner and his golden hair, and thus, the legend was born."

"So are the stories true?" Rory asked. He wanted them to be true, more than anything.

His father smiled. "Some are. But facts have never stood in the way of a good tale."

Hilda shook her head. Izzy sat silently, wrapped up in Goldenrod's history.

"You said you were called away," Rory said. "By who? Where did you go?"

Goldenrod fingered the rim of his mug as he spoke. "There are things in this world that most would think are merely children's stories, Rory. Creatures not known to man. And . . . even more terrible tales." He kneaded his temples with his fingers. "I was on the far side of the globe, where a

241

battle raged for many years. A battle that the folk in Gloom could have never imagined in their wildest dreams."

"A battle," Rory whispered. He remembered what Vincent had said: that a war was being fought, with flames in the clouds and vengeful spirits riding the wind.

"What . . . kind of battle?" asked Izzy tentatively.

Goldenrod inhaled and then blew out a weary breath. "We were at war with a creature known as Mara. Mara of the Shadows."

Panic rose in Rory's throat as the name was spoken aloud. His father eyed him intently. Izzy seemed to be holding her breath.

"A creature," Hilda said, more a statement than a question. She knew what Rory and Izzy had been through.

"Indeed, Hilda. There are . . . things that exist in the dark corners of this world, things best left unseen. Mara is one of them. She is a sorceress."

Rory's mum turned to her son and then back to Goldenrod. When Rory didn't speak, Hilda did it for him. "*Was* a sorceress," she declared.

The mariner leaned back in his chair and locked eyes with Hilda, and then gazed at everyone, as if seeing them for the first time. "*Was?*" he questioned. "Of what do you speak? How . . . ?"

"Me and Izzy," Rory started cautiously. "We . . . I was . . . "

"Arcanus Creatura," Izzy blurted. "They're evil people. A man named Lord Foxglove was one of them. Rory went to work for him as a valet, thinking it was just a job."

"But it wasn't," Hilda said, picking up the thread. "He saw things at the manor. Unnatural things. They tried to beat him! And worse!" A tear sparkled in the corner of her eye, and she angrily wiped it away.

Rory reached out and touched her hand.

A host of emotions played on Goldenrod's features: wonder, anger, and, Rory thought, fear.

"Somehow," Rory said, "they stole the shadows of every person in Gloom. No one knew."

"They don't know it's missing until they look," Izzy said once more.

"And those blasted dark skies hid the sun and light," Hilda added. "It was near dark before noon for the past several weeks."

"But Izzy and I found out about it," Rory said. "We had to stop them." He paused and licked his lips. "I heard Foxglove and the others talking about a great harvest. Me and Izzy figured out that it was probably the carnival folk that came to Gloom, that they were going to harvest their shadows."

"Just like everyone else's in Gloom," Izzy said.

Rory released a breath. The mere memory was painful.

"We found her," Izzy continued. "Mara of the Shadows. She was . . . feeding on shadows that Arcanus Creatura stole for her."

No one had touched the fish stew, which still sat on the stove.

"It all makes sense," Goldenrod said in a faraway voice.

"What?" Izzy and Rory asked together.

"I was called away by my order to stop this very creature. Years ago now. But as the battle wore on, I was captured, locked in a prison not of this world." He rubbed his temples again. "That is why I did not return, Hilda. My companions tried to free me, and it cost them dearly, as they lost their lives in the attempt. But Mara was weakened, and she fled—"

"To Gloom," Rory said.

"A place she had followers," Izzy added, "that could help her regain her strength."

"'My wounds are many,' she told us," Rory finished.

Goldenrod looked at them with wonder in his eyes. "And you stopped her? The two of you? Mere children. How?"

"My shadow," Rory said. "It . . . killed her."

Goldenrod knit his brow. "How?" he asked again, his voice serious and curious at the same time.

Rory absently raised his hand to the chain he once wore, but it was no longer there. "It was in the stone Mum gave me. My shadow."

Goldenrod turned to Hilda and shook his head, as if trying to loosen a memory. "The stone, Hilda," he said urgently, a gleam in his eye. "The one I gave you before I left. I said to always keep it close. Remember?"

Rory's mum blinked, as if awakening from a dream. "I . . . I gave it to Rory. I told him it was something to remember you by."

The sea captain nodded. "It was imbued with strong magic," he declared. "The power of my order. If any harm came to its bearer, the stone would protect them."

Rory thought his father's eyes were glassy, but he couldn't be sure. "So when they tried to steal my shadow," Rory said, finally understanding, "it went into the stone, where it would be . . . safe? To protect me."

"I think that is true, Rory," his father replied.

A long moment of silence descended on the room. Rory saw his mum's stern expression lessen somewhat when she looked at his father. *Perhaps they'll be okay,* he thought. *I hope so.*

Goldenrod looked at Izzy and then Rory, with what Rory thought was respect. "When you defeated the Queen of Sorrow," his father began, "her power was shattered, as well as the bonds of my prison, and I was finally free to sail for home. I'm here because of you, Son."

Son, Rory thought. *He called me "Son."*

Izzy smiled wide.

Rory blew out a breath. He stared at the table for a long moment, then swallowed loudly. He and Izzy had not only saved all of Gloom, he'd rescued his father as well. It was a tale beyond belief, and yet, it was true. But he had one more question.

"You said your order," Rory started. "What order are you talking about?"

A few birds chirruped outside.

"The Order of the Mage."

"Mage?"

"Yes, Rory," Goldenrod said. "I am a mage. And so are you."

CHAPTER THIRTY

The Valet Discovers Himself

A heavy silence filled the room.

"A mage?" Rory finally said.

Goldenrod drew himself up even taller in his chair. "We carry the bloodline of the ancient Sumerians," he said. "The ones who charted the seas of Europica in the cold light of a new world. I was shown the path by my mother, and now you, too, will learn."

Izzy nudged Rory. She was practically squirming in her seat. "See? I knew you had magic!"

Rory was stunned. He turned to his mum. "Did you know?" he asked. "Any of this?"

"No," Hilda said, her face just as shocked as her son's. "I knew nothing of your heritage."

Goldenrod locked eyes with her. Rory saw compassion and regret in his father's gaze. "I did not know you were with child when I was called away, Hilda. If I had, I would have done anything to keep myself close to you."

Hilda Sorenson straightened her back. A muscle jumped along the hard edge of her jaw. "It wasn't right," she said. "I've been here all this time, trying to raise the boy as best as I could. And you . . . you were out sailing the bloody seas!"

Izzy glanced from one adult to the other and shrunk in her seat. Rory watched as pain, anger, and even a tiny shred of joy crossed his mum's face. Her emotions battled one another in front of everyone. Rory didn't know what to say.

Goldenrod cast his eyes down for a moment, then looked back up. "It was not a playful lark, Hilda. I have paid a price for—not . . . seeing my family." He drew his hands together and rubbed the scars on his knuckles.

Rory's mum wasn't moved. "Not even a message?" she fumed. "A letter?"

The great sea captain shook his head and reached for Hilda's hand, but she quickly drew it away. Goldenrod froze. Rory's heart fell. "It was impossible," his father said, his voice filled with sorrow. "This battle was . . . waged on another

248

plane, a place where the rules and laws of time have no bearing."

Rory stirred in his seat. He had so many questions, but it felt as if he should wait until his father and mum cleared the air between them first.

Of course, Izzy filled the difficult silence.

"How many others are there?" she asked. "Like you and Rory?"

It was just one of many questions to which Rory wanted an answer.

Goldenrod sighed. "Some sail with me and a few others are scattered in distant lands. There are not many of us left."

Rory sat still. His mind was racing. He had Sumerian blood.

"The Order of the Mage has existed from time immemorial," Goldenrod said. He shifted his gaze to his son. The son who had saved him. "Rory will learn the path too."

Rory couldn't help but smile, although the air in the room was still tense.

"Not today," Hilda said. "This has all been too—"

"There is much he needs to know, Hilda." Goldenrod leaned forward, his eyes sparkling. "He will need to learn the—"

"*Not* today," Hilda said more firmly.

Goldenrod fell quiet.

It seemed to Rory that his father had suddenly realized just how strange this must be for Rory and his mum. A father, long gone and thought dead, now back home, telling his son he was a mage.

A mage.

"Rest then," Goldenrod said. "I will take refuge at Black Maddie's."

He gave a polite nod and stood up, then walked to the corner of the room and picked up his long wooden staff. Rory got a closer look, and saw that it was engraved with knots and curious marks. Goldenrod glanced at him and then Izzy, and smiled weakly. "I will take my leave."

He opened the door quietly and stepped out, leaving Rory, Izzy, and Hilda sitting in deafening silence.

Rory turned over in bed again and stared up at the ceiling.

His father's words came back to him: *I am a mage. And so are you.*

He still couldn't believe it. What did a mage do? He recalled the old tales he'd heard about mages who went from town to town, performing wondrous deeds. Did he have that power in him now, waiting to be unleashed?

It was all too much.

His father had also said that others had given him the name Goldenrod. So what was his real name? His mum would know. But now he could ask his father himself, he realized.

Rory sighed. Like every child in Gloom, he had grown up with stories of the great Black Mariner and his adventures upon the sea. And now Rory knew the truth. That man was his father. *His father!*

"Tears of a fish," he whispered.

He couldn't pin down his true thoughts. He was happy his father was alive and back in Gloom with him, but it was all so strange and unexpected. And his mum didn't seem very happy about it at all, although he had seen a spark of compassion in her eyes a few times as his father spoke—something that might be kindled and nurtured to bloom again.

Never in a million years could Rory have imagined this turn of events.

He tossed and turned for most of the night, and finally, when he did fall asleep, he dreamed of birds with wings like fire.

CHAPTER THIRTY-ONE

The Path

Goldenrod's arrival in Gloom set the town ablaze with rumors.

War was coming, some said.

It was a sign of the end times, said others.

But Rory knew the truth.

Goldenrod had been freed from a prison conjured by a sorceress known as Mara of the Shadows. Unbeknownst to the town, two children had saved him, one of them being his own son, and the other his son's best friend, Izzy.

The Black Mariner's ship, *Desire,* stayed docked in Gloom and became a magnet for children and other curious onlookers. The crew lodged at Black Maddie's and a few other inns near the docks, and the local proprietors were happy to have new customers who drank as much as they swore.

The chill between Rory's parents had thawed somewhat, but he could see that his mum was still adjusting to it all. She was just as affected by Goldenrod's return as her son was.

Rory was happy that they were finally speaking without so much bitterness. But today, he was nervous.

His father had said it was time to begin his training.

They sat together on a bare patch of ground in the Glades, facing each other, legs crossed. Sunlight filtered through the high trees above them. Birds whistled in the branches.

"Again," Goldenrod demanded. "Focus. Make your mind as empty as a blank page in a book."

Rory looked at the stubby candle planted in the ground before him. He'd been trying to light it for an hour. *With his mind.*

He let out a resigned breath, defeated.

"It took me many years to summon a flame, Rory," his father said, trying to console him. "When one begins to walk the path of the mage, they learn at their own pace, practicing, reading, and mastering their skills until they are ready to attend the Bastion."

"What is the Bastion?"

"It is our institute for the higher mysteries. There, young

mages learn the path. After many trials, if they are successful, they will go through the Ascension. It is the moment when a new mage is initiated into our order and given their own rod of learning."

Rory wondered if that would ever happen to him. "How will I learn all this?" he asked. "This is . . . too strange to understand."

"It will come," his father said, reaching out and laying a reassuring hand on his shoulder.

Rory sighed and nodded, grateful for the encouragement.

The sound of scuttling creatures could be heard in the deeper part of the forest—calls from birds and foxes, the rustling of leaves and of burrowing things.

"A mage gains power from the natural world, Rory," his father explained. "We can summon fire and frost, enchant our enemies with confusion. To walk the path of the mage takes both study and natural ability. It will come," he repeated. "I promise."

Rory couldn't imagine ever being able to summon fire or frost. He picked up a twig from the ground and snapped it.

"Tell me more," his father demanded suddenly. "What else do you remember of this whole terrible experience?"

Rory thought on that a moment. There was one question

he still needed an answer to. "Why did I dream of her?" He balked. "Mara?"

Goldenrod rested his elbows on his crossed knees and made a steeple with his hands. "A mage has many skills, Rory. Some more rare than others. But there is one that we hold in particularly high regard."

He paused, as if Rory would suddenly guess what it was, but Rory had no idea.

Goldenrod closed his eyes. "Tell me, Rory, what am I thinking? What do you see in my mind?"

Rory almost laughed aloud, but his father's expression remained serious.

"Close your eyes," he instructed Rory. "Tell me what you see."

Rory breathed out through his nostrils and did as his father asked. He sat very still within a curtain of darkness for what seemed like minutes. He could hear his own heartbeat pounding in his ears. He was aware of everything around him—the small beetle crawling on his shoulder, a leaf falling from above.

Then, in the darkness, something flickered.

He resisted the temptation to open his eyes and focused on the darkness instead.

Again, a flicker.

Light.

Rory concentrated on it.

"Candle flame!" he shouted. "A candle flame!" He opened his eyes.

His father did the same. "Yes," he said. "I was thinking of a candle. You may not be ready to light a flame with your mind, but you can certainly find it in the void."

Rory could barely contain his excitement. "What does it mean? How did I do it?"

"You have the Gleaning."

"The Gleaning?"

A ray of sun fell across his father's face, highlighting his burnished gold hair. "Some mages have the ability to enter the world between dark and light, Rory. To look into another's mind and read their thoughts. We call them 'dream mages.' You must possess this most rare skill." He paused. "You have the Gleaning, my son."

Rory smiled, excited to discover this newfound talent, but Goldenrod's face suddenly grew grim. "Being a dream mage is a great gift, but it also leaves you vulnerable to attack. Enemies with second sight can find you and read your thoughts and innermost secrets."

Rory tensed. "She could have read my thoughts? Mara?

I couldn't read hers. If I had, I would have known what was happening all along."

"But you *did* read her thoughts," his father insisted, "even in the shapeless form she inhabited. 'I thirst. I hunger.' That is what you heard. Her internal thoughts. Her *desires*."

Rory stared past his father, into the surrounding trees. He had a gift. A secret power.

"But," his father went on, holding up a finger, "there are ways to protect yourself, methods that are taught at the Bastion to cloak your mind from danger."

Rory shifted on the hard ground. *Do I even want to be a mage? What about Mum and Izzy? Does this mean I'll have to leave them behind, like my father did to Mum?*

"I see you're thinking on your future path," Goldenrod observed.

"I . . ." Rory started. "It's just all so much. I had no idea I had this . . . gift, and now I have to decide what I want to do with it."

"Walking the path of the mage is a great honor. It is something that our family has practiced for generations." Goldenrod paused, picked up a stone from the ground, and rubbed its smooth surface with his thumb. "If I had known I had a son, it would have been easier. You would have been raised knowing our ways."

The cry of a hawk sounded in the distance. Goldenrod reached into a bag at his side and pulled something out. He handed it to Rory without saying a word.

It was a small, leather-bound book, and Rory thumbed through the pages. Symbols, letters, and intricate drawings filled the pages. He didn't understand any of it.

"Every apprentice mage receives this book when they begin to walk our path," Goldenrod said. "It contains the secrets of our order. Study it, and commit it to memory."

Rory looked at a drawing of a star with circles on each point. He flipped to another page. The letters looked familiar somehow, like he had seen them in a dream.

"There was something else," he said, pulling another memory from his head. "When I was at the manor, I had to prove to them that I could read. I was given a book, and after I read from it, I was told it was written in something called Old . . . Aramaic? How could I have done that?"

His father raised an eyebrow. "Interesting."

"What?" Rory asked. "What does it mean?"

"That language was lying asleep in your mind, waiting to be awakened."

Rory just looked at him. He was overwhelmed and numb by all he was discovering about himself. Cool air stirred the fallen leaves around them.

"It is called 'transference,'" Goldenrod said. "As a mage, you have the history of our kind lying deep in the recesses of your mind, to be called upon when needed. Our order must have had a mage fluent in Old Aramaic somewhere in our past. For you to already be able to tap into this is indeed remarkable."

Rory felt something stir inside of him, a fire spreading through his whole being.

"Tell me more," he said. "About the order. About what we can do."

The mariner began to speak, and as they sat in the afternoon light of the Glades, Rory heard tales of hidden lands and faraway mountains, of giant squids and sea creatures, of mages who could control lightning from the sky, of men and women who spoke not with their mouths but with their minds, and of the art of using spells to entrance your enemies.

When he was finished, Goldenrod stared at his son for a long moment. "So," he said. "Does that sound interesting?"

Rory grinned. "How far away is the Bastion?"

CHAPTER THIRTY-TWO

Desire

Rory and Izzy sat in their usual spot on the docks at Quintus Harbor.

The mermaid figurehead on the prow of the *Desire* shone in the sun.

A few crew members were on deck, checking knots and polishing the brass ladders and handrails. A white, frothy tide slapped against the hull. A few days earlier, Rory's father had taken him aboard and showed him the gleaming navigation instruments. Rory had run his fingers across the compasses and imagined setting a course for them to sail. He had looked through a spyglass, which extended out in sections and showed distant objects as if they were nearer. But Goldenrod's prize possession was a telescope. It had the same function as the spyglass, but was more decorative and much bigger. It stood on three legs anchored to the deck. "So we can study the stars," he had told him. Rory had seen drawings of these things in books, but to see them on a ship—his father's ship—was pure joy.

Izzy nudged him with her shoulder. "What's wrong? You daydreaming again?"

Rory turned to her. "Just thinking about all this training. It's hard, and I'm not even sure I really want to do it."

"Well, if someone told me I could be a great magician, I'd sign up right away."

"Mage," Rory said.

"What's the difference?"

He shrugged. "Let's say I do all this training and then decide to go away to this . . . Bastion to become a mage." He swallowed. "I wouldn't want to leave my mum and . . ."

"Me?" Izzy said. "Ah, I'll be all right. We had a big adventure, yeah? I can tell people I knew the great Goldenrod and his son, the seafaring magicians. Or mages. Whatever."

Rory shook his head, grateful for the laugh. He was too embarrassed to tell Izzy how much he cared about her.

They sat in silence a moment.

"Maybe I can go too," Izzy said.

"Go where?"

"With you, dummy. To be a mage. I don't wanna read those cards anymore, and my mum would probably say it's okay. She went on a journey herself when she was my age. She said that's how she learned all of her, you know . . . stuff."

"I think you have to have Sumerian blood or something," Rory said, but he wasn't sure. The thought that he was part of an ancient bloodline was too much to comprehend. He scratched his head. "I really don't know, Izzy."

"Maybe they just don't want girls," Izzy said, bringing him back to the moment.

"I don't think that's true." Rory cocked his head in the direction of the ship. A tall woman with dark skin and green tattoos up and down her arms lifted a coil of rope.

Izzy looked at her with admiration and a smile spread across her face.

The sun was setting by the time Rory and Izzy left the dock.

"Stomach's rumbling," Izzy complained as they began to walk.

Rory chuckled. "Doesn't your mum ever cook anything you like?"

"Only if you like vegetables and green stuff." She made a sour face. "I'd rather have fish and clams. And nobody makes better fish stew than your mum."

Rory couldn't argue with that.

They walked by Black Maddie's, where several of Goldenrod's crew sat on barrels outside, regaling the locals with tales of adventure over mugs of ale. A few sailors were locked in arm-wrestling matches with the patrons, a bounty of coins resting under their clenched fists.

In a few more minutes, they passed Market Square, where the Circus of Fates was still drawing crowds. Rory thought for a moment to try his hand at a few games of chance, but reconsidered.

They turned down Copper Street, then walked on to Rory's house.

"Surprise!" a chorus of voices rang out as they entered.

Rory and Izzy jumped back, startled. Rory's mum pulled them in and shut the door.

Rory took in the room. Ox Bells, Vincent, Miss Cora; Izzy's mum, Pekka; Goldenrod, and a few of his shipmates all mingled together in the sitting room. Rory even spotted One-Handed Nick in the crowd. There was barely enough room to hold them all.

"What's going on?" Rory asked.

"Do you know what today is?" His mum grinned at them.

Rory and Izzy looked at each other.

"No," Rory said.

"Well, you and Izzy were both born on the same day. Remember?"

Of course Rory remembered. He just didn't think about it much, growing up in the town known as Gloom.

Pekka joined them. Yellow flowers were braided into her hair. "That's right. We figured it was time for a party. A celebration!"

Rory thought on it. *A party. Why not?*

Izzy smiled beside him.

Vincent approached, walking with his ivory-tipped cane and sporting his monocle. "Rory, my boy. So good to see you. I'll be having a séance in a few days. A very select group. Now that you've seen a few things, you might prove to be a most excellent medium."

Rory was taken aback. "I don't think I—"

"No need to answer now," Vincent cut him off, raising a hand. "Just let me know soon."

He wandered away, leaving Rory looking after him with a dazed expression. Before Rory could trade a glance with Izzy, Miss Cora turned from the conversation she was having with one of Goldenrod's crew, a woman with a long strip of hair that ran down the center of her otherwise bald head. "I can write a play about your adventure," Miss Cora offered. "I'll call it..." She raised a finger in the air as if waiting for some kind of signal. "The Fall of Shadows," she said. She adjusted the hat on her head, which to Rory looked like a strange fish of some sort. "Of course, we'll need to find the right actors," she finished. "Maybe some of the carnival folk?" She sipped from a glass of sparkling liquid.

Rory and Izzy shared a look of befuddlement.

Rory found his father in the crowd and headed toward him. Izzy followed.

"Happy birthday, Son. I'm sorry I wasn't here for the others, but let this be the first of many we spend together."

Rory smiled and then looked down at his feet. He didn't know what to say. Then suddenly, the right words came to him. He looked back up. "It's the first one I've celebrated, so we can call it even and go from there."

His father smiled and laid a hand on his shoulder. "So, have you decided, Rory?"

Rory hesitated. He thought he didn't have to make a decision about attending the Bastion until he was ready.

"Your present," Goldenrod said. "What would you like?"

"Present?" Rory thought for a moment. What did he want?

What had he always wanted to do? "I want to go out on the sea," he said. "A trip, to see some of the world."

"And so you shall," his father replied.

Rory beamed.

"I want to go too," Izzy chimed in.

Goldenrod took a step back, his expression puzzled.

"What?" Izzy said defensively. "I saw a lot of women on your crew. I want to sail the seas with Rory. And go on some adventures."

Rory's father rubbed his chin, considering. "Well, we *could* use someone to help with sails and rigging."

Izzy grinned, giddy.

"The work is hard," the sea captain went on. "Long hours and running lots of errands on the ship."

"I'll have my sea legs in no time," Izzy boasted. "Plus, I have some other skills too."

Goldenrod looked to Rory, who only shrugged and smiled.

"I'm a witch," Izzy declared.

The mariner nodded, a little hesitantly. "Well, I guess I have no choice then, do I?" He lowered his voice. "I don't want to be cursed."

He smiled, and Izzy smiled back.

"No one's going anywhere without me," said Rory's mum,

who had been watching the whole spectacle unfold from a few feet away.

Surprise and delight dawned on Goldenrod's face. "I wanted to ask you," he said to Hilda. "More than anything. But I thought you would refuse."

He took her hand, and this time, Rory's mum didn't bat it away.

"I would dearly love for you to sail with me," Goldenrod said.

Rory looked to Izzy, her face flushed with excitement. "I guess that's settled then," he said. "We're all going!"

And as the fish stew was passed around, they smiled and laughed, and for the first time in a very long time, there was a birthday party in Sea Bell.

The End

Enjoy more creepy stories
by Ronald L. Smith!